The Cowa

The kidnapper had the muzzle of his revolver pressed into Julia's right ear, and the hammer on the gun was in full cock position. It would take only a slight squeeze of the trigger and Julia Branscomb would die.

"You son of a bitch," the skinny kidnapper snarled. "I thought you was dead."

"You tried hard enough," Longarm said. "Damn near got it done. Now I'm putting you under arrest. You'll stand trial for the murder of that stagecoach driver, robbery, kidnapping, maybe for other stuff, too. There will be time enough to think about all that once you're behind bars, which is where you rightly belong."

"Like hell you're taking me in, lawman. Make one move toward me and this girl is dead."

DON'T MISS THESE
ALL-ACTION WESTERN SERIES
FROM THE BERKLEY PUBLISHING GROUP

THE GUNSMITH by J. R. Roberts
Clint Adams was a legend among lawmen, outlaws, and ladies. They called him . . . the Gunsmith.

LONGARM by Tabor Evans
The popular long-running series about Deputy U.S. Marshal Custis Long—his life, his loves, his fight for justice.

SLOCUM by Jake Logan
Today's longest-running action Western. John Slocum rides a deadly trail of hot blood and cold steel.

BUSHWHACKERS by B. J. Lanagan
An action-packed series by the creators of Longarm! The rousing adventures of the most brutal gang of cutthroats ever assembled—Quantrill's Raiders.

DIAMONDBACK by Guy Brewer
Dex Yancey is Diamondback, a Southern gentleman turned con man when his brother cheats him out of the family fortune. Ladies love him. Gamblers hate him. But nobody pulls one over on Dex . . .

WILDGUN by Jack Hanson
The blazing adventures of mountain man Will Barlow—from the creators of Longarm!

TEXAS TRACKER by Tom Calhoun
J.T. Law: the most relentless—and dangerous—manhunter in all Texas. Where sheriffs and posses fail, he's the best man to bring in the most vicious outlaws—for a price.

TABOR EVANS

LONGARM

AND THE
MODEL PRISONER

JOVE BOOKS, NEW YORK

BERKLEY PUBLISHING GROUP
Published by the Penguin Group
Penguin Group (USA) LLC
375 Hudson Street, New York, New York 10014

USA • Canada • UK • Ireland • Australia • New Zealand • India • South Africa • China

penguin.com

A Penguin Random House Company

LONGARM AND THE MODEL PRISONER

A Jove Book / published by arrangement with the author

For information, address: The Berkley Publishing Group,
a division of Penguin Group (USA) LLC,
375 Hudson Street, New York, New York 10014.

ISBN: 978-0-515-15553-2

PUBLISHING HISTORY
Jove mass-market edition / March 2015

PRINTED IN THE UNITED STATES OF AMERICA

10 9 8 7 6 5 4 3 2 1

Cover illustration by Milo Sinovcic.

Chapter 1

"Good morning, sweetheart."

It took Longarm a moment to remember the girl's name. They had had a late and rather wet evening the night before, and he was feeling the effects of it now. Still, he managed a smile for her.

Rita. That was her name. She had red hair, enough tit for two women, and a waist that he could almost reach around with his own two hands.

And reaching around her waist did not seem an altogether bad idea. He settled for the smile and a handful of soft tit.

Rita's nipple responded almost immediately, turning hard and poking into the palm of his left hand as he squeezed.

"Mmm," she said. "This really is going to be a good morning, isn't it?"

"You betcha." Longarm caressed her other tit and gave that nipple a tweak. If he remembered correctly, Rita liked having her tits played with. Last night she had gotten off from him doing no more than sucking her nipple. And the girl flowed pussy juice like a mare giving milk.

"Suck my dick, darlin'," he murmured into the pillowy softness of Rita's left tit.

She giggled and quickly headed in that direction. By the time she arrived, Longarm was erect and ready for her.

Rita peeled back his foreskin and cupped his balls in the palm of her hand while she ran her tongue around the head of his prick.

"Nice," he whispered, his voice throaty and a little hoarse.

"It's a beautiful dick, sweetheart," she said.

"It's not nice t' talk with your mouth full," Longarm said.

"But it isn't in my mouth, sweetheart."

"My point exactly," Longarm told her.

Rita giggled again and dropped her head, engulfing him in the sweet warmth of her mouth. She pushed until she gagged and sucked hard as she withdrew.

Longarm arched his back to meet her and pressed his head against the pillow, lifting his hips to her.

Instead of thrusting, though, he held himself rigid, poised with his hips elevated and his cock buried in the heat of Rita's mouth.

She was able to take nearly all of him, something not too many girls could accomplish. Rita wrapped her lips tight around his shaft and sucked, then pulled back until only the head remained in her mouth. Then she ran the tip of her tongue around and around the head of his cock.

Suddenly she pushed down again. Hard. Taking him deep. Fast. Out again and just as quickly deep.

"Keep that up, darlin', an' you'll get a mouthful," Longarm cautioned.

Rita kept it up.

And she did indeed get the promised mouthful.

Longarm felt the gather and rise of his jism somewhere down in his balls, then the sudden release as it shot up through his shaft and squirted into Rita's throat.

He cried out with the intensity of his pleasure. Rita stayed with him, swallowing hard and fast to keep up with the flow of Longarm's juice.

"Damn but I do like a girl that swallows," Longarm observed.

Rita did not answer. But then she had her mouth full at the time and likely felt it would be impolite to speak.

Only when he was well drained and sucked dry did she finally let his dick slide out from her lips.

The air that suddenly reached his dick was cold on the lingering wetness.

Longarm shivered a little and lightly stroked Rita's back and the cheeks of her rounded ass.

"Nice," he said.

"Nice," she agreed with another giggle.

Longarm sat up. "Now, little darlin', you need t' move"—he slapped her ass hard enough to sting—"so's I can get up. I gotta get dressed and shaved an' whatnot. Unlike some people . . . namely you . . . I can't lay around all mornin'. I got t' go make a living."

Rita fashioned a pout on her pretty lips. "Do you have to?"

"I have to." He added, "An' wipe the cum off your lips." In fact, she had none there, but she could not know that. She wiped her mouth with the back of her hand and moved to make room so he could crawl out of her bed and collect his share of the clothing that had gotten flung around sometime in the wee hours.

He bent, gave Rita a quick kiss, and headed off in search of something to eat before he showed up for work.

Chapter 2

Deputy United States Marshal Custis Long left his boardinghouse, crossed Cherry Creek, and headed into Denver's downtown district, where the marshal's offices were located in the Federal Building on Colfax Avenue.

Long was known as Longarm to his friends. And to a fair number of enemies, too.

He was a tall man, standing over six feet in height, with dark brown hair and a sweeping handlebar mustache. His features were somewhat on the craggy side, and he found them ordinary enough. A good many women, however, thought the deputy more than a little attractive.

He had broad shoulders, long legs, and large, powerful hands, which were gentle with a horse or a woman but could be rough on a felon who made the mistake of resisting arrest.

Longarm wore brown corduroy trousers tucked into black knee-high cavalry boots, a brown-and-white-checked shirt, a brown vest with a gold watch chain stretched between the pockets, a brown tweed coat, and a brown flat-crowned Stetson hat.

His gun belt was black leather and carried its holster just to the left of his belt buckle, the rig canted for a cross-draw.

The revolver riding in that holster was a .45 caliber double-action Colt with black gutta-percha grips and the bluing beginning to wear off from extended use.

Longarm passed the United States Mint and crossed the side street to the Federal Building. He mounted the stone steps and opened the door for a gentleman who was coming out.

He entered the offices of United States Marshal William Vail and tossed a friendly "good morning" to Vail's chief clerk, Henry, seated at his desk outside the marshal's office.

"Incredible," Henry said. "You're only ten minutes late this morning. That may be a record for early arrival."

"There was a long wait at the café this morning," Longarm said cheerfully as he hung his hat on the rack in a corner.

"Sit down and wait," Henry said. "I know the boss will want to see you, but he's busy with some paperwork first, things that have to be done. He shouldn't be long."

Longarm nodded and took a seat on one of the chairs set against the wall. He nudged a spittoon close with the toe of his boot and took a dark, slender cheroot out of his inside coat pocket. He bit the twist off and spit it into the cuspidor, pulled a match from a vest pocket, and snapped it aflame.

He lit his cigar, blew the match flame out, and dropped the spent match into the cuspidor.

Then he sat back, content to wait until Billy Vail was ready to see him.

Chapter 3

"Longarm," Henry said, emerging from Billy's office, his hands full of papers, "you can come in now."

Henry left the door open. Longarm closed it behind him when he went in.

United States Marshal William Vail sat behind his uncluttered desk, the early morning sunshine giving a shine to his bald head.

Billy leaned back in his swivel chair and motioned Longarm toward the two chairs that sat in front of the desk. Longarm accepted the offer and settled into the chair on the right.

"Henry tells me you are just aching for an assignment that will take you out of town for a few days," Billy said.

That was a wild exaggeration. The closest Longarm had come to any such statement was to casually ask Henry if there happened to be an assignment for him. He had said nothing about wanting to get out of Denver. Quite the contrary, he was having a good time in town with the ladies

who were part of a newly arrived dance troupe playing at
the Jasperanza Theater, last night's companion being one
of them.

"You know I'll do anything you need, boss," Longarm
said.

He meant that, too. A great many marshals, political
appointees all, were mere pencil pushers. But not Vail.
Billy had earned the respect his deputies gave him.

Before becoming a U.S. marshal, Billy had been a Texas
Ranger and a good one. Despite his almost angelic appear-
ance, the man was as salty as they came and more than held
his own in a gunfight as had been proven many and many a
time.

"I do have something here that will give you a little
break from city life. Do you know a town called Wyskopf?"

Longarm shook his head. "Never heard of it." He
crossed his legs and pulled out another cheroot, leaned forward to take a match out of the shot glass full of them on
Billy's desk, and lit his smoke.

"To tell the truth, neither had I," Billy said, "but the
town marshal of Wyskopf wired that he has arrested Brian
Henry and wants the hundred-dollar reward posted for
the man.

"What I want you to do, Longarm, is to take the reward
money to this Wyskopf place and exchange it for the prisoner, then bring Henry back here for trial in Federal court."

Longarm nodded. He remembered the case. Henry was
accused of stealing stamps from the post office in Monument, Colorado. That made the theft a Federal crime and
put it squarely in the jurisdiction of Billy Vail and his
deputies.

"Our Henry knows where that Henry is located," Billy said. "He can fill you in on where to go and give you the usual vouchers for meals and lodging. I'm told there is stagecoach service to Wyskopf so you should have no trouble getting there and getting Henry back here. Henry, our Henry I mean, will give you all the details."

"I can leave practically right away, boss. I always keep a bag packed an' ready. All I have t' do is stop by my boardinghouse an' grab it."

"Good. Now go to it, Long. And good luck."

Longarm stood and touched a finger to his forehead in a salute to the boss. Then he went into the outer office to see Henry and get the rest of his instructions.

Chapter 4

There were a number of ways to get to Wyskopf, Longarm discovered, none of them good.

Wyskopf was situated in the Sawatch Range of the Rockies, not far south of Tincup.

To reach it, he could travel through Breckenridge and Fairplay, then down Trout Creek Pass into the Arkansas River Valley and up again to Tincup.

Or he could go south to Colorado Springs and Manitou, up Ute Pass to South Park, and again, down Trout Creek Pass.

Or he could go the longest, but easiest, route by taking a train south to Pueblo then following the Arkansas upriver to Buena Vista and up to Tincup.

Any way he looked at it, this was going to be a long trip to pick up Brian Henry.

Longarm's preparations consisted of buying a fresh supply of cheroots and a bottle of rye to see him through the journey and stopping at his boardinghouse to grab his carpetbag. He left his saddle and Winchester in his room, figuring he would need neither since Wyskopf was served by a coach line.

Everything considered, Longarm opted to take the train as far as he could, it being infinitely more comfortable than the cramped interior of a stagecoach.

He took the afternoon southbound and was in Pueblo not long after nightfall.

When he checked on the Denver & Rio Grande schedule on up the Arkansas River Valley to Buena Vista, the clerk said, "We won't have another heading up that way until morning, Marshal. It leaves at eight ten."

"All right, thanks."

"If you need a hotel overnight, I recommend the Chesterfield. It's just three blocks east."

Longarm touched the brim of his Stetson and picked up his carpetbag, then turned and headed out of the depot.

It was still early in the evening. He had plenty of time to check into the hotel and have something to eat. Then . . . he smiled . . . then he knew of a mighty nice saloon where the rye whiskey was tops, the card players friendly, and the ladies damned good to look at.

He lengthened his stride, eager for whatever the night might bring.

Chapter 5

"This just isn't my night, boys. I'm out." Longarm drained his shot glass and set it on the card table upside down. He pushed back from the table and stood, his knee joints cracking. He gathered up what remained of his cash and dropped the coins into his pocket, then turned and started toward the door.

His way was blocked by one of the waitresses. He had noticed her even though she was not the girl who was waiting on his table. This one had long, light brown hair, high cheekbones, and huge, sparkling eyes. She also had a more than generous bust, which was not hidden by her low-cut blouse.

The girl stepped in front of Longarm and planted her hands on her hips.

"Miss," Longarm said, nodding and touching the brim of his hat. "What can I do for you?"

The girl laughed. "You don't remember me, do you?"

"Uh . . . should I?" And no, he did not remember her,

did not think he had ever seen her before or surely he
would have remembered a girl this pretty.

The laughter turned into a giggle. "I'm Amy."

Longarm's brow knitted together as he tried to remember. "Um . . . Amy, you say."

"Amy Shire." Her laughter rang out again. "Of course,
the last time you saw me, I was fifteen and skinny as a
stick. You helped my family with some problems."

"Shire," Longarm repeated. Then it came to him and he
smiled. "Now I remember. They were homesteading down
south of here. Your father had some problems with a
rancher trying to run him off your land, as I recall."

"That's right," the girl said.

"How is your family now?" he asked.

"Happy. Healthy. Papa proved up on the land this past
year, so they own it free and clear. Thanks to you."

"I was just doing what was right," he said.

"I thought you were the most handsome, wonderful
man in the whole world," Amy said. "I had a terrible
schoolgirl crush on you. I thought about you every night
for weeks and weeks."

Longarm smiled. "It's a good thing I didn't know that at
the time, you bein' only fifteen." He laughed. "And skinny
as a stick."

"I'm not fifteen now," Amy said.

"If you don't mind me sayin' so, you're not skinny anymore either."

"I'm glad you noticed."

"You are?"

"Yes." Amy moved closer and lifted her chin so she
could peer up into his face. "I still have that crush on you,
Marshal."

"I don't exactly know what t' say to that, girl," Longarm told her.

"I can leave here whenever I wish," she said. "And I'm not a virgin anymore. Do you have a room we can go to?"

"Are you sure 'bout this?" he said.

"Oh, yes. I'm sure." She smiled. She had dimples. "Like I told you, I still have that crush on you. But I'm not a schoolgirl anymore."

Longarm hesitated while he worked out the math of how long ago that had been since he was at the Shire farm. Amy would be . . . what? Twenty or twenty-one by now. And she was certainly woman enough. No longer a virgin, she said.

He smiled and offered his arm, then stopped and said, "Do you want to go out on the street dressed like that, or d'you want to change clothes before we go down the street to the Chesterfield?"

"I'll go like this if I wouldn't embarrass you to be seen on the street with me."

"With a girl as pretty as you? I'll be right proud t' be seen in your company, Miss Amy Shire. C'mon now. Let's get outa here."

Chapter 6

Amy was not wearing very much so it took her no time at all to get out of her clothes. She stood before him naked and smiling, not at all shy about showing her body.

And she had an exceptional body to show.

She was slender with a tiny waist, the flat belly of youth, and a generous swell of hip. Her tits were more than a mouthful—considerably more—and stood tall, not needing any support. She had small, nicely formed nipples and pink pussy lips peeping out from a nest of light brown curly cunt hair.

"Do you like?" she asked, raising her arms above her head and pirouetting round and round for his inspection.

"This says I damn well do like," Longarm told her, unbuttoning his fly to expose a raging hard-on.

"My God!" Amy gasped. "I didn't know they came that big."

"Disappointed?" he asked.

"Not hardly. Can I touch it?"

"Sweetheart, you can do damn near anything you like with it."

Amy approached slowly, a feline smile touching the corners of her very full red lips.

She knelt in front of him and Longarm assumed she was about to take him into her mouth. Instead she leaned in close and slowly inhaled, taking in the scent of him. Then she touched him. Very lightly. Very softly.

She peeled back his foreskin and pulled his dick down so she could examine it front and back.

She ran his foreskin up and down as if very gently jacking him off.

Again she leaned close and smelled him. Cupped his balls in the palm of her hand. And smiled.

"Marshal Long, I have to tell you, that's just about the prettiest thing I ever did see," she said.

"Under the circumstances," Longarm said, "I think you could call me Custis."

"Do you know, it's a funny thing, but I wouldn't be comfortable calling you by your first name. I mean, you being my elder and a friend of my father," she said.

"You could call me by my nickname, Longarm," he said.

Amy looked up at him, towering above her, her eyes huge. She smiled. "Longarm. I like that. Like in the long arm of the law, huh?"

"Something like that, yeah."

"All right. Longarm it is." She bounced to her feet, full of energy and enthusiasm. "Now, Longarm, would you please put that pretty thing inside me and give me a good fuck? Please?"

He finished stripping off his clothes and took Amy into his arms. "I'll be glad to," he said, meaning it quite sincerely.

Chapter 7

Half an hour later Longarm lay quiet on top of the lovely girl. He stroked her temple and swept a strand of hair back off her forehead.

"Why didn't you tell me?" he said.

"Tell you that I was a virgin? If I had done that, dear Longarm, you would have been all chivalrous and noble and would have settled for a few kisses. You wouldn't have fucked me, I think."

"No, darlin', I wouldn't have," he admitted.

Amy turned her face to his and smiled. "And that, dear heart, is why I didn't tell you. I've loved you for years and never thought I would be so lucky as to have you be the man who got my cherry."

Her expression grew sober. "Was I all right? Did you like it?"

Longarm smiled and kissed her. "You were wonderful. I more than liked it."

In truth, she had not been exactly wonderful. She had

more enthusiasm than skill. But she was certainly good. And yes, he did indeed like it.

"Did I hurt you?" he asked.

"A little, but it was a good kind of hurt." She wrapped her arms tightly around him and hugged him. "Just knowing it was you that I was with and for real instead of in my imagination . . . it was so very nice for me. Thank you."

Longarm enjoyed the ladies, but it was not just every day that one of them actually thanked him for fucking her. He kissed Amy. And kissed her again. Felt his dick stir and harden.

"Oh!" Amy's eyes went wide. And she smiled. "Really?"

"Really," he assured her. After all, once done, it could not be taken back. The girl was no longer a virgin. Why not enjoy her all the more now that she had taken that big step from girl to woman?

Later Amy was sitting on the side of the bed cleaning herself. "Can I tell you a secret?"

"Of course. Anything," Longarm said.

"Sometimes . . . I've been doing it for years, ever since you were at Daddy's farm . . . sometimes I like to think about you and imagine what it would be like to be with you and . . . and I touch myself. I rub myself down there and it feels so, so good.

"And now I can touch myself and remember. I won't have to settle for imagining."

"When you used your imagination, was it the same as the real thing?" Longarm asked, sitting up and lighting a cheroot.

"Oh, not nearly as good. I didn't know what it would feel like. And I certainly didn't know you would be so big down there."

"If you like," he said, "I can teach you a few things. Like how to take it in your mouth."

"My mouth? Are you serious?"

Longarm laughed and took the girl into his arms again.

Chapter 8

Longarm woke up early and spent more time than he should have pleasuring the now not-virgin Amy. When he realized that time had gotten away from him, he jumped up from the bed and hastily dressed.

"Sorry t' fuck an' run, darlin', but I have a train to catch an' barely enough time t' get there." He bent and gave her a lingering kiss, then straightened and said, "When you see your folks, tell 'em you ran into me. Please give them my regards. They're nice people." He smiled. "An' so are you."

"I'm so happy to be with you, Longarm. Can't you stay a little longer? Can't you take that train tomorrow, for instance? There is so much I want to learn, so much you could teach me."

"I'd love to, darlin', but I'm working, y'know. Maybe on my way back through." He kissed her again, grabbed his carpetbag, and hurried out, glad that the depot was only a few blocks away.

He got there in time to catch the westbound passenger train heading along the recently completed route through Royal Gorge and on to Leadville.

"Tickets. Tickets, please." The conductor, a man with gray hair and a sour disposition, came through the two coaches collecting the printed pasteboards.

Longarm pulled his wallet out of an inside coat pocket and displayed his badge. It was all the ticket he needed. The conductor nodded and passed by.

Longarm looked behind the man hoping to see a butcher boy peddling sandwiches or biscuits or . . . some damn thing. He had not had a chance to grab breakfast before boarding the train.

Not that he regretted spending that time with Amy. He would rather eat her than a dry sandwich anytime. Little Miss Amy was a tasty morsel indeed.

It was amazing—and quite wonderful—how she had grown since he last saw her. Then, just as she herself said, she had been a skinny kid. Now . . . He grinned. Now Miss Amy Shire was far from being skinny. Or a kid.

He did regret . . . a little . . . taking her cherry. She was right about that. If he had known she was a virgin, he would have settled for a little petting but nothing more.

What was done, however, was done, and there was no going back.

And, Lordy, the girl was a quick learner. A quick learner and an increasingly good fuck.

Longarm smiled all the way to Buena Vista.

Chapter 9

"The coach you want is over there, Marshal," the Denver & Rio Grande stationmaster said, pointing. "Tomlin & Nash. With the red stripe and yellow wheel spokes."

"Fancy," Longarm said.

"Handsome," the gent concurred. "Do you need help with your luggage?"

"No. All I have is my carpetbag an' I can manage it on my own, thanks."

"Have a nice day, Marshal."

Longarm ambled over to the waiting stagecoach and tossed his bag up to the driver, who was on top of the rig loading bags. If any. So far, it appeared that Longarm was the only passenger going up onto the mountain.

The driver was a young man probably in his early to mid twenties but with a set of side whiskers that would make a bullwhacker proud. He wore a black slouch hat and had a friendly disposition.

"You need a ticket, mister. Eight dollars. You can pay me before we leave."

Longarm showed his badge.

The jehu grinned and said, "Looks like the line won't be making much this trip."

"I'll be going on through to Wyskopf," Longarm mentioned.

"No, you won't," the driver told him.

"And, uh, why is that?"

"Because this coach don't go to Wyskopf. We go through Saint Elmo and on up to Tincup, but there's another line that has the Gunnison to Wyskopf run. You'll change to their coach in Tincup."

"I didn't know that."

The man grinned again. "Anything you want to know, Marshal, just ask me. I'm full of useless knowledge and maybe a little bullshit so I can make up whatever I don't actually know."

Longarm laughed and climbed into the coach. It was a fairly light vehicle being pulled by a six-horse hitch, suggesting there was some serious climbing ahead.

Fortunately, he thought, negotiating these mountain roads was not his concern, and the driver looked like a man who, despite his youth, knew what he was doing.

"Wake me when we get there," he called up to the jehu.

"Oh, you'll know. By the time we pull into Tincup, you and any other passengers we might have will be praising the Lord and kissing the ground."

Two other passengers showed up and came inside the coach with Longarm before the driver made a last call, then removed the hitching weights from his leaders and climbed on top.

He cracked his whip over the ears of the leaders, and the coach lurched into motion.

Chapter 10

Longarm had no idea how Tincup got its name, but he had always liked the tiny mountain community. When he and the other passenger—one man left the coach at Saint Elmo—climbed out of the coach, it was dark and cold and windy.

Sounds of revelry came from one of the saloons close to the Tomlin & Nash office.

Longarm stepped inside, thinking he should have brought a winter coat despite the midsummer time of year. It was damned cold at this elevation. He did not know how high Tincup was, but it was high enough that he could feel a difference both in the temperature and in the slight difficulty in breathing at this altitude.

"Help you, mister?"

"I'm needing to transfer, I understand. I need t' get to Wyskopf," Longarm told the clerk.

"You need the Gunnison Line for that, mister, but their coach won't be through until tomorrow morning sometime.

They don't keep an office here, but they've made arrangements for us to take care of their passengers in addition to
our own. I can go ahead and sell you a ticket now if you
want to take tomorrow's coach."

"Thanks, but that won't be necessary. Is there a hotel
where I can stay the night?" Longarm asked. The place
where he had stayed the last time he was in Tincup had
burned down, or so he'd read in the *Rocky Mountain News*
some months back.

The clerk nodded. "There's a decent place over on Wal-
nut Street. They're clean."

"Quiet?" Longarm asked.

The man chuckled. "There's no place in Tincup that's
quiet," he said and motioned with his chin toward the
nearby saloon.

"Then clean will have t' be enough for me tonight,"
Longarm said. He thanked the man and walked over to the
Placer Heaven Hotel.

The impression he got was that the Placer was about as
much whorehouse as it was hotel. But at least the saloons
with their noise were a good block away so he should be
able to get some undisturbed sleep.

Or so he thought.

Chapter 11

"Up! Everybody up!" a man in the hallway shouted several times over.

Longarm came awake with a sudden sense of dread. Shouting like that in the middle of the night generally meant fire. Fire was the scourge of these mountain communities. Not only were the shacks generally built lightly, but virtually none of the smaller towns had public fire departments. Even larger towns often had only one paid professional in their fire department; everyone else was a volunteer.

Longarm grabbed for his clothes and scrambled into them quickly while in the hallway outside his room the unknown sentinel continued to shout for everyone to get up and get out.

As soon as he had enough clothes on to cover the important bits, Longarm snatched up his gun belt and buckled it over his drawers as he headed for the room door.

The man doing the shouting was burly with a black beard and the red-veined nose of a drunk.

Which, in fact, the fellow was. He reeled from side to side as he continued to roar.

"There's no fire?" Longarm asked another resident of the Placer, who was standing in the hallway in his small-clothes.

"Nah, it's just Jesse, drunk and celebrating."

"Celebrating?"

The local man grinned. "Anytime Jesse finds a nugget, he thinks it's cause to celebrate. That'd be all right, but it sure makes it hard for a man to get any sleep when he comes to town."

"Shee-it," Longarm grumbled.

He marched down the hall and tapped the big man on the shoulder.

Jesse turned to face him, and Longarm said, "I'm gonna put this as polite as I know how, mister. *Shut the fuck up!*"

Jesse gave Longarm a long, slow looking over from toe to head and back again.

Then the big man balled up his fist and let fly.

Chapter 12

Longarm swayed to his left, letting the fellow's right hand fly past. Longarm countered with a right hand of his own aimed at the point of the man's jaw.

It missed, thudding instead atop Jesse's ear when he tried to draw back.

The big man dropped into a crouch and growled— Longarm was not sure at first what he was hearing, but the noisy son of a bitch actually growled—before he tried a looping left hand.

Longarm ducked under that and came up inside the big man's reach, tattooing his gut with a flurry of lefts, rights, and lefts again. Hitting that belly felt like hitting a clapboard wall. There was practically no give to the bastard's flesh.

Even so, Longarm thought he might have found a weak spot because the man grunted with each blow that landed.

Longarm slid to his right and chopped a hard right hand into Jesse's short ribs, driving the air from him and making him turn pale, although whether from pain or lack of breath, Longarm could not tell.

Jesse connected with a right that came out of nowhere and landed on the shelf of Longarm's jaw, dropping Longarm to his knees. The big man moved in and tried to knee Longarm in the face, but Longarm fell back, off balance, arms flailing.

Longarm righted himself and drove upward, sending a crushing right uppercut into Jesse's belly. The big man grunted and doubled over. Longarm saw the opening and smashed Jesse on the side of the jaw, dropping him to his knees.

Longarm finished it with a right hand that pulped Jesse's nose and probably loosened some teeth.

Jesse toppled over, blood running from his nose and mouth, breath ragged and heaving.

"Now," Longarm said, "I will repeat myself. Shut the fuck up an' let people sleep."

He turned and headed back to his room, unfortunately wide awake now.

Up and down the hallway he could hear some clapping, presumably from men who also wanted to be able to sleep without further disruption.

Longarm bolted his door behind him, not at all sure that Jesse would not want to come for him later that night, and had a jolt from his traveling bottle of rye whiskey to help him calm down and get back to sleep.

There were no further disruptions that night.

Chapter 13

Longarm had time enough for breakfast and a visit to a barber before the Gunnison coach to Wyskopf pulled in. He was able to watch the street from the barber's chair and, when he was finished, had a smooth shave, a mustache trim, and smelled like a garden flower.

"We'll get there before nightfall, Marshal," the driver told him. "Else we'll not get there at all."

Longarm was not entirely sure what the driver meant by that remark.

Then they took the road to Wyskopf, and though for the most part it was a perfectly ordinary route, he eventually understood the driver's comment.

The road climbed, dipped, and wound back and forth. There were places where Longarm was fairly sure a mountain goat would lose its footing and tumble off the narrow track, which squeezed a road between a sheer rock face on one side and a drop of several hundred feet on the other.

"How the hell did they build this?" Longarm asked the man when they finally arrived and the few passengers left the coach.

"You mean back there at those drop-offs? I guess that part was a real bitch to build. You might not have known it at the time, but for a little way there, we were driving over places where there was no ledge to put the road on so they built a sort of ledge. Built it out from the cliff face with timbers spiked or drilled into the mountainside and rock filler piled on top of them. They say there was more than one man who lost his life working on that road, but they had to have some way to get the gold ore out.

"The mine owners got together and pitched in to pay for that road. I suppose it was worth the effort and the cost, else they wouldn't have put their money into it." The man shrugged and offered Longarm a chew off his tobacco plug.

Longarm thanked the man for the information but declined the offer of the chew. He pulled out a cheroot and lit that instead.

"Any idea where I can find the town marshal?" he asked.

"Over there, I think," the driver said, pointing to a hardware and mining supply store across the narrow street. "I think the fella that runs that store acts as town marshal when one is needed."

"One last thing an' I'll quit bothering you. Can you direct me to a good hotel?" Longarm said.

"Far as I can tell, Marshal, there isn't any such thing as a good hotel in or around Wyskopf, but personally I always stay at the Elkhorn. It's down the street two blocks on the left."

Longarm thanked him again and picked up his carpetbag.

The stagecoach would not be returning to Tincup until morning so he figured to first check into the hotel for a room, then look up the town marshal of Wyskopf and see to his prisoner.

Chapter 14

His room at the Elkhorn was a cubicle, bare except for a narrow cot—army surplus equipment, Longarm suspected—and a washstand in one corner and a lantern hanging on the wall. For this he was charged three dollars a night. If the government had not been paying for it, Longarm would have bought a blanket and slept outdoors.

At least the one-person cot assured him he would not have to share the room. Or the bed. With a stranger. He had been in that situation many a time in the past and could deal with it but much preferred some privacy.

It took only a few seconds to assess the room and shove his carpetbag beneath the cot. He took a close look at the lone blanket that was folded at the foot of the cot. It was not especially clean and that was acceptable enough, but he did not want to host a gathering of bedbugs overnight.

There seemed to be none. For that he was grateful.

Longarm yawned and stretched, scratched his balls, and went out in search of Brian Henry and the town marshal.

Marshal Ezra Keene was a merchant, a member of the town council, and the grand high poobah of one of the feathery fraternal orders. Longarm could not keep all of those straight in his mind . . . and did not particularly want to.

"Oh, yes. Marshal Vail sent a wire saying I should expect you," Keene said when Longarm introduced himself. "You're here to collect the prisoner and, uh . . ."

"And t' give you the hundred-dollar reward for nabbing him," Longarm finished for the man.

"I was hoping I could have that now," Keene said.

Keene was about forty years of age, medium height and build, and bald as a boiled egg. The mining supply store he owned seemed prosperous enough, and his clothes were nicely cut, but there was something about his eagerness to get that reward money that Longarm thought a little odd.

Perhaps the man gambled or was addicted to laudanum or to a grasping whore, Longarm speculated.

Not that any of those would matter. He had Brian Henry locked up and was entitled to the reward.

Longarm reached into his pocket and pulled out a small coin purse. He handed it to Keene, who rather too quickly snatched the purse, opened it, and looked in at the five lovely gold coins it contained.

"Paid in full," Longarm said, "but if you don't mind, I'll leave Henry wherever he is until that stage pulls out tomorrow. And, um, come to think of it, where is he now?"

"I have him chained up in a shed out back," Keene said.

"A shed?" Longarm said.

"Well, actually it's more like an outhouse," Keene said. "It stinks kind of bad but it has a roof over it. I put a lock on the door so nobody can get in to him, and he couldn't get out even if there was no door."

"Can I see?" Longarm asked.

"Sure. Let me get my key."

The key was in Keene's cash box. The hardware store owner motioned for Longarm to follow and led the way out a back door to the outhouse.

He was certainly right about one thing. The small structure did indeed stink. Longarm could smell it even before Keene unlocked the door and opened it to expose Brian Henry to the fading sunlight.

Henry blinked and shielded his eyes against the sudden rush of light.

The prisoner was wrapped in chains, shackled hand and foot and sitting on one of the two open holes of the shitter.

Brian Henry looked more like a store clerk than a criminal. Or like a postal clerk, which was what he had been in Monument, Colorado, before he was caught pilfering stamps from the drawer.

He was small and thin, with spectacles perched on the bridge of his nose. He had mouse brown hair that needed cutting and a scrawny excuse for a beard that failed to hide a weak chin.

He looked like the sort who would steal stamps three cents' worth at a time.

Still, the government wanted him back for trial and likely for a term in prison. Longarm guessed he would draw a sentence of two or three years, but an example had to be made that it was just plain stupid to steal from Uncle Sam.

"You all right in there, Henry?" Longarm asked.

"Who are you, mister?"

"Deputy marshal. I'll be taking you back to Denver t' stand trial. We'll leave in the morning," Longarm said.

"Thank God. At least that will get me out of here," Henry said.

"You can stand it one more night," Longarm told him, then nodded to Keene, who shut the door and locked it again.

As they walked back to Keene's store, the man asked, "Can I be reimbursed for his meals while he was here? And maybe for the cost of that telegram I sent to Marshal Vail?"

"I have some forms in my bag at the hotel," Longarm said. "I'll bring you one in the morning when I collect the prisoner. You can fill it out an' mail it down to the marshal. It isn't up to me if they pay you or not."

"But you think they will?"

Longarm shrugged, then asked, "You wouldn't know where a man can get a good meal, would you?"

Chapter 15

Longarm had a mediocre supper at the recommended café, highly overpriced as was to be expected in an isolated mining community, then he wandered into one of the town's saloons for a some poor-quality whiskey at twenty-five cents a shot.

When he mentioned that to the man standing next to him at the bar, the fellow snorted and said, "Mister, that isn't the worst of it. There's only three whores in town, and they're all ugly."

"Forgive me for sayin' so, but I'm mighty glad I live down to Denver, where the whiskey is good an' the whores are good to look at. The ugly ones can't make a living so they quick enough catch on to the lay o' things and move on," Longarm told the man.

"I'd move on myself," his friendly neighbor said, "but the money here is too good to pass up."

"Good wages?"

"I'll say. I have to pay six dollars a day," the man said.

"You have to pay . . ."

"I own the Primrose Mine."

"You have my sympathies," Longarm told him and bought the man a drink.

The coach back to Tincup was supposed to leave at sunup so Longarm turned in early. The canvas cot in his room was hard. But not as bad as sleeping on a slab of rock, which he would have had to do if he moved outside into the chilly night air. And the blanket was scratchy but warded off that chill.

All in all, he was grateful for a solid night's sleep. He woke early, better rested than he would have expected, and quickly washed and dressed.

He wolfed down a quick breakfast of porridge and coffee and took a cruller with him to collect Brian Henry in case Marshal Keene had not given the prisoner any breakfast.

As it happened, Henry had eaten before Longarm got there so Longarm ate the cruller himself while Keene unlocked the maze of chains he had used to secure the woebegone little clerk.

"All right, Brian. Time t' head back down an' face the music," Longarm said as the prisoner emerged from his odiferous place of confinement.

"What are they going to do to me?" Henry asked.

"That ain't up to me," Longarm said, exchanging his own set of handcuffs for the light chain Keene had used. "All I'll do is get you there. From there, well, you know the rest."

"I didn't take much," Brian said. "I'd be glad to pay it back."

"An' so you will," Longarm said, snapping the cuffs around the man's wrists. "One way or another."

Longarm thanked Marshal Keene and motioned for Brian to come along. "We have us a coach t' catch."

Chapter 16

The road was narrow, but the mules pulling the light coach were accustomed to the route and were steady. Driver Hugh Taylor trusted them completely even on the worst stretches where a misstep could lead to disaster.

Taylor snapped his whip well above the long, floppy ears of his off leader—he would rather have had the whip taken to his own back than to touch one of his mules with it—and the coach began moving.

Unlike one of the big Concords, the Gunnison Line mud wagon had nothing to speak of in the way of springs so it bumped and shuddered over the rough roadway, but it did not sway from side to side very much and his passengers rarely became seasick.

Half a day to Tincup, then down to Gunnison, then two days off while John White took the outfit back on the Gunnison to Wyskopf run. With his own four-up. Taylor would not have allowed anyone else to drive his beloved mules, never mind that they belonged to the company. They were *his*, by godfrey, and no one else should even think about driving them.

They reached the bad patch about an hour into the run. The road was beginning to crumble just a little under the traffic. Taylor made a mental note to mention that to someone back in Wyskopf the next time he was there. Someone needed to repair the shelf before it got any worse from the constant grind and weight of the ore wagons passing over it.

A bull team pulling an empty ore wagon approached on its way back south, but there was a pullout next to the rock wall wide enough for the bull team to move out of the way while the coach passed on the outside.

The bullwhacker saw Taylor and waved. He guided his team aside and made sure the back of his wagon did not intrude into the roadway.

Taylor let his mules ease ahead. They were perilously close to the drop-off, but he knew they were steady.

Just as the near leader reached the lead bull, the rust red ox snorted and gored Taylor's mule in the ribs.

The mule, startled, shied violently to the right, bumping into the off leader.

The off mule was bumped aside.

Its feet hit the edge of the road and slipped over it.

The mule brayed and tried to throw itself back onto the road, but too late.

It fell, screaming, and took the other three in the hitch with it and the coach behind them.

"Dear God!" Hugh Taylor cried.

The man's last thought was for his mules rather than the four passengers who were inside the coach.

Chapter 17

Longarm felt the coach lurch, then tip, then with a great screaming of man and mule alike, fall free off the side of the mountain road.

Foolishly, instinctively, he threw himself over Brian Henry in a vain attempt to protect his prisoner.

His impressions of the next few seconds were fragmented and disjointed, mere glimpses of awareness and uncertain impressions. His shoulder driving into the midsection of the passenger sitting opposite him inside the coach. A sprig of mountain laurel slashing him across the face as it whipped into the window opening and was instantly gone again. The sounds of splintering wood and screaming men.

Thuds and thumps and a dull, hollow bang inside his own skull and something hard contacted the crown of his head.

And then . . . there was nothing.

As Longarm drifted away from the world, there was nothing except blackness and pain and intense cold.

Chapter 18

Cold. Frigid. Shivering, his teeth chattering, Longarm became dimly aware that the whole left side of his body felt like it was freezing.

And it was dark. His eyes were closed but he could tell that it was dark. Or so he thought.

Was he dying? He was not yet dead; he was sure of that. And he was determined he was not damn well going to die either.

But, Lord, he was cold.

Longarm gasped for breath. Moaned aloud. Tried to decide if he was dying.

"Marshal? Are you . . . I mean . . . you're alive."

"Henry?" He managed to get it out on the third try. "What . . ."

"You been out of it, Marshal. I really thought you were dead," Brian Henry said.

Longarm tried to concentrate, tried to work out where they were and why he felt so terribly cold. It took him a long moment for the truth to sink in. He was lying in the wreckage of the Gunnison Line's coach. Apparently they had come to rest in a creek, because there was a flow of icy cold water moving through the wreckage.

Longarm lay on his left side, which was immersed in the cold water. Had been for hours. He was sure of that because it was night now. It had been fairly early in the morning when the wreck occurred.

"Henry?"

"Right here, Marshal."

"Are you all right?"

"Banged up some but nothing's broken," Brian Henry responded.

"What about the others?" Longarm tried to sit up. He could not. He could feel nothing along his entire left side. Even that ear hurt.

"Dead," Henry said.

"What about you?" Longarm asked. "Why'd you stay all this time?"

Henry managed a laugh. "I stayed right here, Marshal, because I didn't have a choice. You shackled me, remember? The chain is caught in some of the wreckage. I didn't move because I can't."

"Can you reach me?"

"I think so," the prisoner said. "Should I?"

"Help me out of this water. I can't seem to move."

"I'll try." A minute later Longarm heard, "All right. Now what?"

"Here. Give me your hand. Try an' drag me out o' the water."

Now that his eyes were open and he was paying attention to what little he could see, Longarm was aware of stars in the night sky overhead and of a soft glow of moon-light as well.

He saw Brian Henry's arm reaching out to him. Long-arm grabbed hold of the smaller man's hand and heaved. With Henry's help, he was able to sit up.

"Now push me over toward your feet," Longarm instructed. He fished in his vest pocket for the key to the locks that held Brian Henry captive in the wreckage.

"What . . ."

"Just do it, all right?"

"If you say so, Marshal."

"And bring your left foot up as close to me as you can get it," Longarm said. "Yeah, like that."

He fumbled the key into the hole, very nearly dropped it, then managed to get the lock open. That shackle fell away. The right leg gave him less problem.

"Jesus," Henry said, rubbing his ankles. "Thank you."

"Now help me out of this mess, will you?"

Brian Henry stood, stomped back and forth getting circu-lation back in his legs. He returned and stood over Longarm.

There was nothing to hold the man there any longer, and Longarm could do nothing to stop him if he chose to bolt. Which any sensible felon should surely do. Longarm would not even hold it against him if Brian Henry chose to flee.

Longarm supposed he could shoot the man. Supposed that he should shoot him if he tried to escape. Knew he was not going to shoot anyone, not for such a petty crime as Henry had committed.

Chapter 19

With Brian Henry pulling and Longarm pushing with his one good leg, they managed to get Longarm out of the wreckage and onto the dry creek bank.

"Lordy, that's better," Longarm said, rubbing his left hand and arm, trying to get some feeling back into them.

"Obviously we need a fire," Henry said. "Come daybreak, I'll gather some dry wood." He laughed. "If nothing else, we can burn what's left of the coach. It can't be useful for anything else."

Longarm dipped two fingers into a vest pocket and brought out a pair of Lucifers. He tried to snap one aflame but got nothing but a little soft material on his thumbnail for his trouble.

"D'you have any dry matches?" he asked.

Henry looked up from the tiny pile of broken slats and splinters that he was collecting by the light of the moon and the stars. "No, Marshal, I don't smoke."

"What about the driver or that other passenger?"

"I'll look," Henry said.

He stood and picked his way over to the wreckage. Longarm lost sight of him in the shadowed darkness, and for a moment Longarm thought the prisoner might have taken that opportunity to slip away now that he was free of the shackles.

After several minutes Henry returned, splashing through the cold water of the creek. He shook his head.

"The driver's body is caught underneath a dead mule. The passenger doesn't appear to have been a smoker. I couldn't find any matches, dry or otherwise."

"All right, thanks." Longarm thought for a moment, then said, "Come morning, we can look for my carpetbag. I have matches in there. In the meantime, I guess we dry out slow."

"And cold," Henry added.

"Yeah. That, too," Longarm said.

"Is there anything else I can do for you, Marshal?"

"No, I . . . I can't think of anything." He snorted. "Nothing short of a nice fire, maybe a bottle of rye and a juicy steak."

"As soon as I can figure out how to get those for you, Marshal, I'll make the arrangements," Henry said.

"Yeah, well, I know I been sort of sleeping for this entire day, but truth is, I'm tired. Cold or not, fire or not, I'm gonna lay down here an' see if I can get some sleep."

"Yes, sir. Guess I'd best do the same. Tomorrow might be a long day."

"G'night, Henry."

"Good night, Marshal."

Chapter 20

In the gray, watery light of dawn, Longarm looked up at the mountainside they had tumbled down and marveled that the two of them were alive.

The drop was almost but not quite sheer. If it had been a straight drop down several hundred feet from the road above, they would surely have died. As it was, there was a slight, a very slight, slope which they rolled, slid, and bounced down.

The coach had come completely apart and now lay in splinters, mostly in the cold water of the creek at the base of the mountain.

"Seems incredible that anybody could live through that, don't it," Longarm observed.

"We almost didn't," Brian Henry said, shuddering. "Marshal, there is something I want from you, please."

Longarm raised an eyebrow and waited for the man to go on.

"I'd like to borrow your pistol for a minute." Henry

grinned. "I know. Here I am, your prisoner, and I'm asking for the loan of your pistol."

"Can I know the reason for that, um, that rather odd request?" Longarm said.

"One of those mules over there is still alive, Marshal. The poor thing is suffering. I want to put it out of its misery."

Longarm grunted. And handed over his .45. Henry was staying with him even though he could have walked away at any time and Longarm would not have been able to stop him. Yet he stayed.

In addition to handing his Colt to his prisoner, however, Longarm surreptitiously palmed the derringer he customarily carried in a vest pocket. Oh, he believed Henry. But just in case . . .

Instead of making a threatening move with the borrowed pistol, the former postal clerk waded back into the water of the creek, leaned down, and pressed the muzzle of the Colt against the forehead of a still breathing but terribly broken mule. The sound of the gunshot was muted.

Henry came back to where Longarm was lying and returned the revolver, handing it over butt first. "Thank you, Marshal."

"Thank *you*, Brian," Longarm said, marveling both at the fact that he had given the gun to a prisoner to begin with and that the prisoner had then chosen to return it. He slipped the derringer back into his vest pocket without Henry noticing.

Longarm opened the loading gate of his Colt and punched out the empty brass, reached into his coat pocket, and slipped a fresh cartridge into the cylinder.

It occurred to him that he had only a handful of cartridges as spares in case of sudden need, but he had matches and a box of cartridges in his carpetbag, wherever that was.

"Brian, can you find my carpetbag, please?" Holding his hands out to indicate the size of the bag, he said, "It's about this big, and—"

"I know what it looks like, Marshal. I saw when you put it on board, remember?"

Half an hour later Henry returned empty handed to report, "Sorry, Marshal. I can't find it anywhere. It must have landed somewhere up on the mountain, but I can't see it up there. It definitely isn't anyplace down here that I can get to."

"All right, thanks."

Longarm pulled out his spare cartridges and counted them. Eleven. Plus the five that were in the revolver. He hoped they did not have to get into a fight down here, not with man nor beast.

He returned all but one of the squat little cartridges to his pocket, then brought out his folding knife. He got Henry to hold the one cartridge while Longarm very carefully used the knife blade to prize the lead bullet out of the brass casing.

"Bring me a handful of dry grass, please, Brian, an' some splinters. I'm gonna see if I can make us a fire."

When the nest of tinder was ready, Longarm sprinkled the gunpowder from the empty cartridge case onto it, then loaded the case with its unfired primer into his revolver. He spun the cylinder to put the empty case under the hammer, held the muzzle several inches away from the waiting gunpowder, and said, "Pray that this works, Brian." And pulled the trigger.

Chapter 21

Longarm removed his coat and opened his vest so he could better feel the heat coming off their fire. They were mostly burning what was left of the stagecoach. The dry, lacquered wood burned quickly but gave off a good heat.

He was beginning to regain a little sensation in his left hand and arm although his left leg remained useless. The return of feeling was not altogether pleasant as it now felt as if a thousand pins and needles relentlessly jabbed his flesh. If he'd had any laudanum, he would have taken some to dull the painful sensations. As it was, all he could do was grit his teeth and bear it.

"We need t' eat," Longarm said, leaning closer to the fire.

"I'm hungry, too," Henry said, "but in case you haven't noticed, we don't have anything *to* eat."

"Brian, I'd say we got a couple thousand pounds o' fresh meat laying right over there," Longarm said, pointing toward the creek and the wreckage it contained.

"Are you serious? Mule meat?"

"Sure. Indians eat it. It don't hurt them none. Won't hurt us either, 'cept maybe our feelings. And it sure as hell won't hurt the mule. All o' them are already dead." He fished his knife out and handed it, still closed, to Brian Henry.

"Cut strips o' meat, not steaks. They're easier t' handle on a stick since we don't have no good way to handle a thick cut o' meat," Longarm told his skeptical prisoner.

Henry made a sour face. But he took the knife, opened it, and walked back into the cold water of the nameless creek. He stopped and looked back at Longarm. "Are you sure we want to do this?"

"Ayuh, I'm sure."

With a sigh of resignation, Brian bent to the task. Ten minutes later he and Longarm sat holding improvised skewers with eight-inch-long strips of meat dangling from them.

"I'll give you this," Brian said at one point. "The stuff does smell awfully good. It is making me even hungrier than I was before."

Longarm barely cooked his before starting to eat. Brian let his nearly burn. By the time he began to eat, Longarm was already cooking his second piece.

"I have to admit it," Brian said half an hour later, "mule meat is not that bad. It is all a matter of becoming hungry enough, I suppose."

"Then I reckon I was hungry enough," Longarm said, wiping his hand on his trousers and smoothing his mustache. He smiled. "For a prisoner, you ain't such a bad sort."

"If all jailers are as decent as you have been toward me, then I have little to fear," Brian said.

Longarm grew sober. "You'll be treated hard in prison, Brian. It's only fair that you know that."

"I don't really expect it to be pleasant. Nor easy," Brian said. "There is no point in running, though. You or someone very much like you would catch me eventually anyway, and I already discovered that I don't like being on the run. I was looking over my shoulder constantly. It wasn't a comfortable freedom. Better to get this over with and put it behind me than to live in anticipation of it."

"Good," Longarm said. "The sentence won't be forever." He smiled again. "Might feel that way at the time, o' course. But you'll get through it."

Longarm said nothing to Brian about it, but his intention was to have a long talk with whoever prosecuted Brian and perhaps with the judge as well. He intended to ask for a measure of leniency for him. If permitted, he would speak on Brian's behalf at his trial.

But none of that could happen until they got back to Denver. At the moment, with his leg not working and limited use of his left hand, that prospect seemed a long way off.

"Shove another piece o' that meat onto my stick here, would you, please?" he said, changing the subject.

Chapter 22

Brian walked to a thicket of pine trees a hundred yards or so distant and collected an armload of pine needles, brought them close to the fire, and went back for more. When he had a good pad of needles, he opened one of the suitcases he found in the wreckage and pulled out the clothing it contained. He laid the clothes over the pad to create a bed and hauled Longarm onto it with his near-frozen side toward the heat of the fire.

"No, turn me around the other way, please," Longarm told him.

"But it's your left side that frozen," Brian said.

"Yeah, but if I got frostbite an' warm up too quick, I could get the gangrene. Could even lose the leg." He smiled. "I'd just as soon not do that, so it'd be best t' warm up slow. You might not'ta noticed, but I been sitting with my good side toward the fire. There's a reason for that."

"Oh, sorry. I didn't know." Brian shifted Longarm around

so that he was lying in the other direction, with his good side toward the warmth of the fire.

He scrounged through the wreckage again and found a greatcoat that might have belonged to the dead passenger and brought that back. He used it to cover Longarm from chin to knee.

"Is that better?"

"Sure is, thanks," Longarm said. "Now if you'd just go find me a feather pillow . . ."

Brian got up and took a few steps toward the wreckage in the creek, then stopped and turned to face Longarm, gaping at the absurdity of the request. After a few seconds he caught on and began to laugh. "Coming right up," he said.

"We don't know how long it'll be until a search party finds us or my legs gets better an' we can walk out, so just t' be safe, Brian, why don't you cut us some more of them mule steaks. Cut a good supply an' wrap them in cloth an' sink them in the creek to keep cold. That should stop the meat from spoilin' too quick."

"All right."

Longarm noticed that once he got into the creek, Brian was doing more than cutting meat off the mules. He was scavenging the body of the dead passenger, too. A little while later he came back to the fire carrying two bundles.

"What's those?" Longarm asked, watching Brian drop the bundles beside the fire. They were wrapped in what looked to be someone's shirts.

"I got to the driver's body. I cut our meat from the mule that was lying on top of him and managed then to roll it off the man. I went through his pockets and the other fellow's, too. These are their things. There's some money, watches and watch chains, that sort of thing. I don't know who they were but they're apt to have family who should get these things."

"And the shirts?"

"Out of a suitcase."

"Still no sign of my carpetbag?" Longarm asked.

Brian shook his head. "Sorry. It must be up on that mountain somewhere." He smiled. "And before you ask, no, I'm not climbing back up that damn cliff to look for it. Coming down that thing once was quite enough for me."

Longarm dropped his head back against the pine needle bed Brian had made for him. "Damn, I hate feelin' so useless. Good thing for me that you've stuck around when you could've run."

"You need me," Brian said, adding wood to the fire. He stood and brushed himself off. "I'm going over there to find some more wood and bring it back, so don't think I'm running now. I won't be far. If you need anything, just shout."

"Y'now, Brian, as prisoners go, you ain't so bad," Longarm said with a grin.

"I'll bet you say that to all your captives," Brian said, laughing. Then he trotted off in search of more wood for their fire.

Chapter 23

"Marshal! Look!" Brian jumped to his feet, grinning and pointing to the south, back toward Wyskopf.

"I can't see nothing," Longarm said.

"Oh, right. You can't stand up to see. Marshal, we're saved. Some men are coming."

"How many? Does it look like a search party or what?"

"It's . . . I don't know what they are. It's two men on horses. They're definitely coming this way. They're following the creek."

"Maybe they can help," Longarm said, "or anyway send somebody that can."

"They are a mile or so away. They should be here in a half hour, I think." Brian was still excited, Longarm pleased enough but not exactly jumping up and down about it even had he been able to.

As a precaution, Longarm slipped a sixth cartridge into his revolver and returned the Colt to his holster beneath the greatcoat that covered him like a blanket.

Brian saw and asked, "You're expecting trouble?"

Longarm smiled. "Let's hope not, but it pays t' be ready anyhow, just in case."

Brian stared toward the men, then said, "Should you be putting me back into handcuffs or something?"

"Why? You goin' somewhere I don't know about?"

"I mean, well, I *am* a prisoner and all that."

"Nah. No need." Longarm smiled. "I woulda been in a helluva fix here if it wasn't for you, Brian. I'm not gonna put you in 'cuffs at this late date, not just for showin' off to some people I don't even know. Anyway all that is between you an' me. Nobody else needs t' know about it."

"If all my jailers are as tolerant as you . . ."

"Don't count on it. Those riders are definitely coming our way?"

"They are. If nothing else, they surely can see the smoke from our fire. They have to know that we're here," Brian said. He seemed excited. "Do you think you could ride double with one of them? With your leg like it is, I mean. I could walk alongside. Or they could put you on a horse and one of them walk."

"You're counting your chickens before they're hatched, Brian. Let's see what these fellas think before we go making ourselves free with their horses."

"I know, but—"

"It's okay," Longarm said. "I understand. But we don't wanta take advantage. We don't know how friendly they are, so wait an' see."

"Even so . . ."

Longarm smiled at Brian Henry's excitement. He himself was content to wait and see how things turned out.

Chapter 24

The two men came at a slow, steady pace. As they neared, Longarm could see that the man who was slightly in the lead was squat and swarthy, with a black spade beard and wearing a cloth cap. The other was of medium build with dark red hair, clean shaven, and bare head.

The men reacted to Brian Henry's shouts of both joy and invitation. They rode near then dismounted without a word and walked into the cold water of the creek.

They sifted through the wreckage, stopped over the bodies of both passenger and driver, and riffled through the pockets of the dead.

They found a brown valise and opened it, dumping the contents that they rejected and pocketing several items which Longarm could not see, perhaps money, perhaps something else that they found to be of value.

Only when they had thoroughly searched the wrecked stagecoach and the dead passengers did they emerge from the creek and approach Brian Henry and Longarm.

"You been through all that shit over there," the dark man said. "What'd you get?"

"It doesn't matter," Brian told the two. "Their personal possessions will be sent to their families if we can find them."

Both newcomers laughed.

"Did I say something funny?" Brian asked.

"You sure as hell did," the smaller man responded. "Because you see, we'll take whatever you got off of them if you please."

"And if we don't please?"

"Then you'll be just as dead as them, and we'll take their shit anyway," the big man said.

"And yours, too, of course," the smaller one put in.

"You can't do that," Brian yelped.

"You got a gun? You gonna stop us?" The two had themselves a good laugh again.

The men became serious. "All right, that's enough," the dark one said. "Hand it over."

Both intruders pulled their pistols.

Longarm spoke for the first time. "Boys." He coughed, turned his head, and spit, then cleared his throat and tried again. "Boys. You shouldn't ought t' do this."

"What's the matter with you, bub? Stand up," the big one said.

"Yeah," his pal added. "What's the proper word for that?" He snickered. "Stand and deliver."

"I'd stand up t' face you if I could," Longarm said. "As 'tis, I'll have t' fight you layin' down an' with one hand tied behind my back. So to speak."

"*Fight* us? You'll die where you lie, asshole."

"Maybe not," Longarm said, smiling.

Chapter 25

"Uh, Tim?" the smaller man said nervously. "Lookit that son of a bitch, Tim. He's smiling. The man shouldn't ought to be smiling."

Tim, the squat, dark man with the heavy beard, looked puzzled. "You aren't afraid to die, pilgrim?"

Longarm continued to smile. "Oh, I might be. When my time comes. But the day I can't take down a pair of pissants like you is the day I deserve t' die."

"You, uh—"

"This thing poking up underneath the coat? It ain't a hard-on, boys. It's a Colt .45. An' I'm a deputy United States marshal. This man here is my prisoner. Now, lads, I would consider it t' be a mighty friendly thing was you both to unbuckle your gun belts an' let 'em drop."

He waited. Watched. Smiled again. "That's nice, boys. Good of you to cooperate. Now back away from those guns. Thank you. Brian, would you be so good as t' pick those belts up an' bring 'em over here. Thank you."

Longarm swept the greatcoat off to reveal his .45. "See, boys? I wasn't lying. Brian, please bring their horses over here. Thank you."

"Now, fellas, I am not stealing your horses, but I am confiscating them. Temporarily. In the name o' the Fed'ral government. You can pick 'em up again in Wyskopf. I'll leave them at the livery for you.

"Brian, hang those gun belts on the horns o' those saddles if you would, please, then lead 'em over here and help me up into a saddle. I don't think I can do it by my own self."

Getting the horse over to Longarm was no problem at all. Getting Longarm onto the horse was another matter entirely. In the end they had to enlist the help of both Tim whatever his name was and his partner. They had to manhandle Longarm up and into the saddle.

Neither would-be robber made any move toward the revolvers and gun belts that were hanging from the saddle horns. But then they did seem acutely aware that Longarm's leg did not work but his gun hand seemed to work just fine, and that big Colt was never far from his hand.

Eventually, however, Longarm was on one horse and Brian Henry was mounted on the other.

"Which way is it to Wyskopf now?" Longarm asked.

The one called Tim pointed. In the wrong direction.

Longarm laughed and said, "I'm not that easy fooled, boys. I just wanted t' see which way you would try and send us. C'mon, Brian. Let's go see if we can find our way back to civilization, or what passes for it up here, without any more trouble."

He reined his mount back toward Wyskopf, nearer than Tincup, and another attempt to return to Denver for Brian's trial and incarceration.

Chapter 26

Longarm tied up outside Ezra Keene's mining supply store. "Come along, Brian," he said.

"What about these pistols, Marshal?" Henry asked.

"Oh, uh, leave 'em there for now, I guess. They ain't going anywhere," Longarm said.

"How about your leg? Do I need to find some crutches? I don't think I could carry you."

Longarm smiled at the thought of little Brian trying to lug his lanky ass around Wyskopf. "No need. My leg is startin' to wake up a little. Feels like a got a swarm o' bugs in there, every one o' them trying to devil me. And doin' a pretty good job of it. But I think I can use it. A little. Just stand close so's I can lean on you, if you don't mind. Now come along. We need t' find Marshal Keene."

"Yes, sir." Brian Henry followed Longarm inside Keene's store. Before they found the man, Brian leaned close and whispered, "You aren't going to make me sleep in that outhouse again, are you?"

"No, I reckon we can make other arrangements," Longarm told him.

He spotted Marshal Keene at the back of the store arranging some stock. The man seemed very surprised to see them walk in. He rushed to them and grabbed Longarm by the shoulders, a gesture Longarm did not particularly care for although he said nothing to the man about it.

"You're alive," Keene bubbled.

"Seems that way."

"I already wired Marshal Vail that you were dead."

"Then I expect I'd best unwire him, hadn't I." Longarm yawned and scratched his balls. He could use a good meal. And a good sleep. "When will another coach leave for Tincup?" he asked.

"The replacement came up last night. It headed back down this morning, so I'm afraid you are stuck here for two nights," Keene said. "A coach will come up tomorrow and go back down again the next morning. Unless you want to hire someone to take you out. It would be expensive but it could be done."

Longarm shook his head. "No need t' put that much on the gov'ment's bill. We can stay over in the hotel, I expect. What about grub? Where's the best eats in town?"

"Same place as before," Keene said. "We don't have all that much to choose from, and most of them are pretty raw."

"Fine dining in comparison t' what we been doing," Longarm said. "But no matter. The café will be just fine. And a room at the Elkhorn again."

"Do you want my chain and shackles for this jailbird?" Keene asked.

"No, not this time, but I thank you for the offer." He turned, leaning rather heavily on Brian, and headed back outside.

First the hotel, he thought, to make sure they had a place for the night, then supper.

Chapter 27

"I don't know 'bout you, kid, but I'm bored," Longarm said. They were in the room at the Elkhorn. Longarm had had the proprietor bring a mattress pad in for Brian to sleep on rather than lock him in Ezra Keene's outhouse again.

They had had their supper. Both had bathed in a wash-house not far from the Elkhorn. Now there was nothing to occupy them for the next two evenings, and Longarm was wanting to walk off the pins and needles sensation that was making his left leg a pillar of agony.

"Grab your cap, Brian."

"Where are we going, Marshal?"

Longarm grinned. "Out."

With a shrug, Brian Henry picked up the cloth cap he had hung beside Longarm's Stetson and slapped it onto his head. "Ready when you are, Marshal."

Longarm led the way down the block and around the corner to a saloon that was more casino than drinking establishment.

"I'm gonna play some cards," Longarm said. "Make
sure you stay behind me. I wouldn't want anyone t' get the
idea that you're there to read the other fellas' hands and
make signs to me."

"People would do that?" Brian asked.

Longarm gave the postal clerk—*former* postal clerk,
actually—a long look. "You'll steal a three-cent stamp, but
you don't know that men will cheat at cards if they think
they can get away with it?" He shook his head. "Brian, you
are somethin' special. I swear I never ran inta anyone like
you before."

"I took more than three cents, Marshal," Henry said
indignantly. "I took nearly a thousand dollars." Then he
rolled his eyes and said, "Oops. I don't know if they know
that yet. That I got away with so much, I mean. Obviously
they know that I stole from them."

"Mind if I ask you something?" Longarm said.

"Anything."

"Why?"

Brian hung his head and stared down toward the toes of
his shoes. "A woman," he said after a long pause.

"We're all susceptible," Longarm told him. "She took
the money an' dumped you once she had it?"

"Yes, sir. Exactly."

"That is a lesson we all have t' learn, one way or
another, Brian. O' course in your case you're learning it an
awful hard way. Prob'ly three to five years' worth o' hard,"
Longarm said. "But what's done is done so leave it be an'
learn from it. Now come on. Stick with me, but a step or
two behind, while I play some cards."

Chapter 28

Longarm heard the commotion and turned to see. A large man had left his seat at one of the tables and had Brian by the throat. Literally. With the fingers of a large and powerful-looking hand wrapped around the clerk's throat. Brian was turning a dark red above the neck and seemed not able to breathe.

"Excuse me, gents," Longarm said. He closed his hand of cards and laid them facedown on the green baize.

Longarm stood and took a long stride to stand next to Brian. "Something wrong here, mister?"

"This little son of a bitch's been jinxing me, watching my cards, maybe passing signs about what I got in my hand, making me lose," the belligerent fellow said.

"With all due respect," Longarm said, smiling, "this man is with me, not with anybody at your table, and I'm pretty sure he doesn't know enough about poker to know what's good and what ain't. So let him go before I get pissed off. Which is something you really do *not* want."

"Listen, bub, you can mind your own business here. My business is with this little bastard."

"Mister, you are hurting him, and he happens t' be under my protection. So leave him be. If you have a beef, take it up with me, not him."

Brian's complexion had gone past red and was rapidly approaching purple. His legs had begun to sag so that it was the man's powerful grip on his throat that was holding him upright.

"I told you nice," Longarm said, "but you wouldn't leave it be." He balled up his fist and let fly.

The fellow absorbed a straight right to his jaw. It was a punch that would have floored most men. Not this one.

It did, however, have the effect of getting him to let go of Brian's throat. The little clerk fell to the floor, gasping for breath. But at least he was breathing, Longarm saw.

It also had the immediate effect of transferring the fellow's anger from Brian to Longarm.

"You son of a bitch!" he roared.

And threw a left hook that would have rattled Longarm's brains if it had connected. Instead, Longarm swayed back and let the fist fly past, close enough and hard enough that he could feel the breeze from its passage.

Longarm stepped inside what he expected would be a right and ripped a right, left, right combination to the fellow's gut. It should have dropped the big bastard to the floor puking his guts out. At the very least it should have doubled him over. All he did was wince a little and back away from the punishment.

Fortunately for Longarm, the man was powerful but slow. He drew his fist back and tried again.

Longarm tried to move lightly back from the punch.

His bad leg betrayed him, buckling and tossing him off balance and into the path of the blow.

The punch was a body shot. It felt like it broke a rib. The pain shot hard through Longarm's midsection.

"All right, damn you," he snarled.

He moved in close again and slammed the palm of his left hand onto the big man's forehead. That rocked his head back and exposed his throat. Longarm drove his fist, knuckles forward, hard into the fellow's throat.

It was a blow that could have crushed the windpipe and made it impossible for him to breathe, as in "ever again." Fortunately for both men, it did not kill. But it certainly stopped his breathing for the moment. And all the more so when Longarm drove a vicious right high beneath his ribs, knocking out what breath remained in him.

The man staggered backward and dropped heavily onto the chair where he had been sitting at the card table.

"Had enough?" Longarm barked.

Mutely the fellow nodded and waved it quits.

"Jesus, mister. You beat Charlie Gaspar? Jesus!" a man at Longarm's table said. "We didn't think that could be done."

"All you all right, Brian?" Longarm asked, reaching back and helping Brian to his feet.

"Yeah. Sure. Uh, thank you, Marshal."

Longarm felt his aching ribs and shook his head. "Say, kid, why don't you go t' the bar an' get us each a shot o' rye." He smiled. "That should ease the aches some."

"Yes, sir."

Longarm handed Brian a half-dollar to pay for their drinks and turned back to his cards. "Sorry for the interruption, gentlemen."

Chapter 29

With several shots of good rye whiskey under his belt, Longarm slept well that night. When he woke up in the morning, Brian was already awake and sitting on his pallet.

"Are we heading back down to Denver today?" Brian asked.

Longarm shook his head. "The Gunnison coach will come up this afternoon sometime. We'll head back down on it tomorrow morning." He grinned. "So we got another day t' kill up here." He yawned hugely and stretched, scratched himself, and stood.

"How is your leg today, Marshal?"

Longarm stamped his left foot a few times. And smiled. "Better. Way better today. Get yourself dressed. We'll go get us some breakfast, see what kind o' trouble we can find t' get into today."

Both dressed quickly and went out into the bright morning sunshine of another day.

"Breakfast first," Longarm said, leading the way to a café that looked a little cleaner than most they had seen in Wyskopf. The food there turned out to be expensive. But then everything in the isolated mountain community was pricey, having to be hauled up from Gunnison or from Buena Vista and the railroad in the other direction.

"Now what?" Brian asked after they ate.

"Now we head to that barber shop I seen in the next block over. We got plenty of time so why not use some of it?"

Longarm stood treat for haircuts and shaves for both of them, splashes of bay rum included, then took them out into the sunshine on the street again.

"I don't know about you, Brian, but I can only think of three ways t' kill time in a town that ain't your own." He grinned. "And sleeping ain't one of them."

"What do you have in mind then?" Brian Henry asked.

"First off, I got t' ask for your parole. I know how you been acting. You could've run off when I was down in that creek freezing my balls off, but you didn't. I expect I can trust you not to run now, but I got t' hear it from your own mouth. Do I have your promise?"

"Of course you do," Brian said. "I take it you aren't going to chain me in Mr. Keene's outhouse again?"

Longarm laughed and slapped the small man on the shoulder. "Not hardly." With a smile he added, "While I was in that barber chair, I asked the man a question. Got an answer, too. An' now, Brian, you are gonna go with me to one of the pleasures of a mining town. That is, they never close. Men coming off the different shifts will have their needs an' wants met an' never mind what time o' day or night it happens to be."

"I have no idea what you are talking about, Marshal," Brian said.

"No." Longarm laughed. "But you will. Come along now. I know where we're gonna spend our time waiting for the coach down to Tincup."

Chapter 30

The house was exceptionally nice, a clear cut above most of the places in Wyskopf. It was tall and narrow, at least three stories, and ran deep from the road.

"What's this?" Brian said as they let themselves in through the low gate into the bare patch of ground that passed for a front yard.

Longarm did not answer except to wink as they mounted the steps onto a wide but shallow front porch. There were none of the usual chairs on the porch.

Longarm tugged a bell pull. Presumably it rang somewhere in the house although they could not hear the sound from outside.

There was a delay of half a minute or so, then the door was answered by a pretty mulatto girl wearing a black dress with a white apron over it. "Come in, gentlemen, please, sirs."

Brian looked up at Longarm and asked, "Is this, uh . . ."

Longarm laughed. "Yes, 'tis."

"But I can't afford——"

"My treat, Brian," Longarm said. "I likely wouldn't be

here if it hadn't been for you helpin' me back there. I would've laid there in that creek until I died. I owe you. An' you are fixing t' go behind bars for the next few years. There won't be no pussy where you're going. If anything, there's apt t' be rough sons of bitches looking to poke you in the ass. But this, Brian, this is your last chance t' have a woman, so pick you a good one. Two if that's what you want."

Longarm turned to the maid and said, "I need t' talk with the madam o' this fine house, miss. I got some arrangements to make for me an' my friend here. You see, we expect we'll be spending the day here an' all night, too, so her and me need to talk some.

"Then we'll want t' have a look at the girls so's we can pick an' choose what looks good to us.

"What I hear is that you got the best-looking girls in these mountains, so trot 'em all out for us to see, will you. But first, I want t' talk with the madam in charge o' this house."

The girl dropped into a curtsy and bobbed her head. "Right away, sir."

"Surely you can't mean—"

"Oh, but I do. My treat. Whatever girl you want. Or girls. Just pick 'em."

"What about you?" Brian asked.

"Hell, I want t' stay someplace warm an' comfortable while we wait for that coach. You ain't the only one. So I reckon I'll pick me a girl t' stay with, too." He laughed. "The only question I have is, how'm I going to put this down on my expense account?"

"Marshal! You wouldn't," the little man gasped.

Longarm laughed again. "No, I wouldn't. But it's fun t' think about, i'n't it?"

They were interrupted by the arrival of the madam.

Chapter 31

It was expensive, Longarm thought. But worth it. Besides, he had some poker winnings in his pocket so in a way it was like they were spending someone else's money.

"Bring out the girls, Wanda," the madam in charge of the house ordered once negotiations were complete and Longarm had paid the tab for the two of them to spend the day—and the night—while they waited for the next Gunnison Line coach to Tincup.

At this unusual hour there were only four girls working, and if they were the best that Wyskopf had to offer, Longarm felt sorry for the men who lived there.

To someone from Denver, they seemed a poor lot. But they were not in Denver now.

The girls were wearing Chinese silk wraps with dragon designs. The wraps extended barely below the waist and were tied to emphasize their busts.

Brian turned to Longarm and whispered, "Were you serious about . . . you know?"

"Actually I don't know what you're asking me. Spit it out plain an' I'll answer you," Longarm said, using a normal speaking voice instead of a whisper.

Brian cleared his throat and hesitated for a moment, then said, "About me taking two girls?"

Longarm laughed. "Kid, if that's what you want, just pick 'em, they're yours."

"How do I . . ."

"You mean you never been in a whorehouse before?" Longarm asked.

Brian shook his head. "Never."

"Just tell the madam which ones you want. Or point to 'em if you're too shy t' ask outright."

Brian pointed. He chose a thick-bodied girl with bleached hair and huge tits and a girl with brown hair and the second biggest tits. Obviously Brian was a tit man, Longarm thought.

That left two for him to choose from. He took his time deciding, then settled on a skinny girl with red hair and no discernible tits. He would have taken the other except for some pock marks on her face that made him think she might have a communicable disease, and that he did not want.

The redhead smiled—she had a genuinely lovely smile—and came to him.

"My name is Trudy," she said.

"Short for Gertrude?"

"No. Just Trudy. What is your name?"

He told her and Trudy took his hand. "Come with me, Custis. We're going to have us a fun time."

Chapter 32

Trudy slid the bolt on the door, turned, and untied the sash that held her kimono together. She let the silky garment slide off her shoulders and kicked off her slippers, standing before him wearing nothing but a smile.

Longarm smiled back at the girl and took her into his arms. He knew he was not supposed to kiss her—you never knew where that mouth had been—but she was such a delightful girl that he kissed her anyway.

Trudy leaned back a little and looked up at him. "That was . . . that was sweet. Thank you, Custis."

He kissed her again, then stepped back and quickly stripped his clothes off.

Trudy started to come to him, but he held a hand up to stop her. "Wait. Let me look at you," he said.

She seemed puzzled, but she obeyed.

Trudy was of medium height, with dark red hair cut short. She was not a classic beauty, but there was something about her that Longarm thought set her off from the run of the herd. She had a joy in her, something special that shined through from within.

Physically she was slender, with small tits—tea saucers rather than teacups—and sharply prominent nipples that just begged to be sucked. She had a flat belly and a thick bush of dark, curly hair with her pussy lips peeping out from within that nest.

Her legs were slim and pretty.

And her smile. Trudy had just about the nicest smile he could remember seeing for many a day.

Longarm laughed and took her into his arms again, enjoying the cool, smooth feel of her naked body against his. Enjoying the way she fit into his embrace. Trudy molded herself to him and wrapped her arms around him.

"I think," Longarm said, "this is going to be a delight."

Trudy lifted her face to him, and he kissed her.

Without him asking, she dropped to her knees. She lightly petted his dick and peeled the foreskin back. She spent several moments just looking at what he had. He could feel Trudy's breath warm on the shaft of his cock.

Then, so lightly he could scarcely feel it, she ran the tip of her tongue up the length of his dick and around and around the head of it.

Longarm took a deep breath. "You know," he said, "you're driving me crazy down there. Take the damn thing in your mouth, will you?"

Trudy laughed. And continued to tease his prick.

Finally she leaned forward and took him into the warmth of her mouth.

And in. And in.

Longarm could not believe how deeply she could take him. His dick was uncommonly big, but Trudy took him deep, past her mouth and into her throat until he could feel her chin nudging his balls.

It was not just every girl who could handle him like that, and he loved the sensations Trudy was giving him.

When she pulled back, the air was cool almost to the point of feeling cold on his now wet cock.

Trudy took care of that for him. She wrapped the fingers of one hand tight around his shaft and pulled, tugging him down onto the bed. Down onto her.

Chapter 33

"Yes . . . hard . . . hard . . . you can't . . . hurt me . . . like this . . . harder, sweetie, harder."

Longarm pounded Trudy's belly with his own, his cock ramming into her deep and hard, his every thrust driving the breath from her in small, explosive puffs.

Trudy wrapped her arms around him and clutched him to her with her legs as well. She clung to him, her small body demanding pleasure. And giving it.

She latched on to the side of his neck with her teeth. He knew she would leave a mark. A badge if not of honor then certainly one of passion.

"More . . . yes . . . harder." Trudy's hips rose to meet his every thrust, her passion at least as great as his, at least as demanding.

Longarm drew his head back and clenched his teeth. His back arched and his limbs trembled. With a powerful, final thrust he came in a rush, a great outpouring of cum that spewed hot into Trudy's pussy.

Trudy reached her own climax. She cried out aloud and bit his shoulder.

He collapsed on top of her, spent. But only for the moment. He had her services all day and all night, too, and he intended to enjoy every moment he was with her.

Trudy smiled and kissed him and poked him in the ribs.

"Hey! What was that for?"

"Roll off of me, honey."

Longarm shrugged and rolled to the side and onto his back.

"Now lie still."

"All right."

Trudy shifted around so that her head faced toward the foot of the bed. She bent low and cupped his balls in the palm of one hand while with the other she lightly toyed with his dick, wet with his cum and her pussy juices.

She dipped her head lower and took him gently into her mouth.

"You do know how t' please a man, don't you," he mumbled.

While Trudy sucked, his dick responded, filling out to a full erection once again and still she sucked. And then she began to hum. Slowly, softly, the sensation growing in intensity until he was not sure he could take it any longer.

He reached down. Took her by the shoulders and tugged.

Trudy pulled away and laughed. She knew good and well the effect she was having on him. With his cock standing hard and tall again, she quickly straddled him, one knee on either side of his body. She impaled herself on him and began to rock back and forth, in and out.

Longarm closed his eyes and gave in to the pleasure Trudy was giving him.

Chapter 34

"Tired?" she asked, her voice muffled some by the fact that her nose was pressed somewhere in the vicinity of Longarm's left armpit.

"Yeah," he admitted. "A little." It was sometime in the early evening, and they had been screwing like minks all day.

Trudy popped up and kissed his nipple, then sat upright on the side of the bed. "Would you excuse me for a minute?" she asked.

"Sure." Longarm did not bother to open his eyes. He felt the bed shift a little when Trudy stood, and he heard her bare feet on the floor.

He heard the rustle of cloth and looked up in time to see Trudy tie the sash of her kimono, unbolt the door, and leave. Longarm dropped his head back onto the stuffed pad that passed for a pillow and closed his eyes again.

A minute or two later—it could not have been very long—he heard the door open as she returned, this time carrying an empty basin and a kettle. Steam escaped from the spout of the kettle that dangled from her hand. She was smiling.

"You're awake. Good. Get your lazy ass out of bed and come over here for a minute."

More curious than obedient, Longarm got up and walked, naked, over to the girl. He leaned down and kissed her. And this time he *did* know where that mouth had been. And where he wanted it to be again very soon.

"None of that now," she chided.

"Why?"

"Just hush and do what you're told," Trudy said.

"Bossy little thing, aren't you."

"Yes, but I'm cute. And a pretty good fuck if I do say so myself."

"I won't quarrel with that," Longarm said. He reached for her, but Trudy slid out of his grasp. "Really, Custis. Just stand there for a minute or two."

"Yes, ma'am. If you say so." So he just stood there.

Trudy set her basin on the washstand and poured hot water into it. From beneath the stand she produced a cup of soft soap and a washcloth. She dredged the cloth into the hot water, took a two-finger dab of the soap, and worked that into the cloth.

Then, starting from his face and neck and frequently returning to the basin and soap, she began washing him, head to foot, all the while humming a tune. He did not recognize what she had in mind for the music, but he certainly enjoyed the feel of the bath she was giving him.

When he had been thoroughly soaped up all over, including in the crack of his ass—"I intend to have my tongue there in a little while and I want it to be clean, if you don't mind"—she poured the now soapy water into the thunder mug, poured fresh water in, and set about rinsing him all over, including in the crack of his ass.

"You, little darlin', are a jewel," he said. And he meant it.

"Hush," Trudy said. "Go back to bed and get some rest. I'm going to wash myself and then we can fuck some more. Go on now. Scat!"

Longarm scatted.

Chapter 35

"What the hell is that?" Longarm sprang bolt upright on the bed. Somewhere in the house the late-night peace was being disturbed by screaming and the crashing of furniture being broken.

Longarm and Trudy had been dozing off and on, but that was not possible with all that noise.

"That doesn't sound right," Trudy said. "Usually this is a quiet house, not at all like this."

They heard a gunshot and then another. Longarm jumped out of bed, stepped into his balbriggans, and grabbed his .45. "Stay here," he told Trudy. "Don't even peek out. I'll let you know when things are okay."

He kicked aside the remains of their late-night supper and padded barefoot to the door and silently slid the bolt back, then opened the door a crack and peered out.

In the hallway outside the next-door room was a large man, nicely dressed. He looked more like a manager or a mine owner than a working stiff. He was almost certainly drunk and had one of the girls sobbing at his feet. The girl was on her knees and was bleeding from the nose and mouth. Her face was puffy from crying. The man had her by the hair with one hand. In the other he held a revolver.

"Shut your fucking mouth, bitch, or so help me, I'll put a bullet behind your ear. Try and steal from me then, cunt. Just try it when your stupid brains are sprayed all over this wall."

The man yanked the girl's head back and shoved the muzzle of his revolver into her mouth.

Longarm stepped out into the hallway. "Hey! Tough guy. You're able to whip little girls. Want t' try it with a grown man?"

The fellow turned around and blinked. "Go away. This bitch stole my money. I'm gonna get it back from her or take it out of her stinking hide. And I don't need any help from you, thank you."

Longarm fashioned a smile and walked forward. "What are you gonna do to her?"

"Gonna beat the living shit out of her, that's what."

"Can I watch?"

"I don't need no help."

"Oh, I don't want to help. I just want t' watch."

The whole while Longarm was talking, he was inching closer to the belligerent drunk. And closer. The man seemed not to notice until Longarm was standing immediately at his side.

"No, you can't watch. I'm going to beat her fucking brains out, but that's just for me to see. You understand?"

"I understand," Longarm said, still smiling. Without looking down, he shifted his grip on his .45 so his hand was wrapped around the cylinder and he was holding it upside down. Held that way, the butt made a dandy cudgel or billy club.

It served that purpose again as Longarm's arm came up and he smashed the flat butt against the drunk's temple. The fellow folded up like a wet towel dropped onto the floor.

Longarm reached down and plucked the revolver, a nickel-plated Ivor Johnson, out of the unconscious man's hand. To the still-sobbing girl, he said, "You might want t' get out o' the hallway before this asshole wakes up."

"You didn't kill him?" the girl asked, looking up with unspilled tears glistening in her eyes.

Longarm shook his head. "No." He grinned. "But he'll have himself one helluva headache tomorrow."

"You should have killed him," the girl snapped.

"You can if you like, but I ain't going to," Longarm said.

"Dumb bastard spent all his money. I didn't steal none of it."

"I believe you," Longarm said. "Now if you'll excuse me." He tried to touch the brim of his hat toward her, only to discover that he was not wearing the hat.

He turned and went back to the room he was so pleasantly sharing with Trudy, at least for a few more hours. After that, he would never see Trudy again, which at the moment seemed quite a shame. She was one hell of a girl. One hell of a fine fuck, too.

Now that the danger was past, the corridor was beginning to fill with gawkers milling about in various stages of undress. Longarm left them to whatever they cared to make of the situation and went back to his own pursuits.

He grinned at Trudy when he returned to their room. And bolted the door closed behind him.

"Since we happen t' be awake . . ."

She came into his arms. She felt almighty good there. It seemed a pity he couldn't take her back to Denver with him. That being so, however, he should make the best of what time he had left with her.

He took Trudy by the hand and led her back to the rumpled, sweaty bed.

Chapter 36

"Now what?" Longarm mumbled. He had been dozing, half asleep, lying on top of Trudy after depositing another wad of cum into the girl. Now someone was tapping at the door.

The fellow from the corridor? If so, that was going to be one sad, sorry son of a bitch when Longarm got through with him.

Longarm rolled off Trudy and stood up, yawning and stretching and reaching for his .45. No more using it to whack the bastard with the pistol butt, though. If he thought he was going to intimidate Longarm, he was very much mistaken. And would pay for that mistake.

Longarm unbolted the door and stepped well to the side, then leaned close with the muzzle of his revolver leading the way, and pulled the door open just a crack.

Instead of seeing the drunk, however, he found himself confronting—and obviously terrifying—the same young mulatto girl who had answered the doorbell to let them in the day before. The girl was staring wide-eyed and frightened into the muzzle of Longarm's .45.

"I . . . I . . . I j-j-j-just w-want to s-see Miss Trudy," she stammered.

"Oh, jeez, I'm sorry," Longarm said, dropping his arm and pulling the door open.

The visitor seemed not to notice that Longarm was naked. She rushed to the bedside and leaned down, whispering something to Trudy. Then, as quickly as she had come, she scurried out into the now empty hallway.

Longarm closed and bolted the door then returned to the bed. Trudy, he noticed, was suddenly pale and not at all her usual exuberant self.

He sat on the side of the bed and gently stroked her shoulder. "What's wrong? Why'd that girl come here?"

"It isn't important," Trudy said in a small, distant voice. She was crying, he saw, and trembling.

"Like hell it wasn't," Longarm said. "Tell me."

She sighed. "There's nothing you can do about it, so don't worry."

"Kid, you look scared. And that girl didn't come here for no reason. It has t' be something important. Please tell me."

Trudy squeezed her eyes closed and turned her face away from him. "I'm scared," she whispered.

"Scared of . . ."

"Vicky is a friend. The best friend I have in this place. She wanted to warn me. She heard the boss tell Jake Bramley . . . he's the man you got into it with out in the hallway . . . she heard him tell Jake that he could have me tonight and do whatever he wants with me.

"Jake is one awfully mean man. He hurts the girls bad and there's a rumor that he killed a girl once. He went too far with a beating and she died. He likes to hurt the girls. He had me once before, and I couldn't walk right for almost a week after.

"Vicky said Jake is mad because you beat him and everybody saw, so now he wants to take it out on one of the girls. And she said it will be me. Jake will be back tonight, after you've gone." Trudy broke down in sobs, her tears coming hot now.

Longarm stroked her back and turned her over so he could take her into his arms. He smiled at her. "Don't you worry, lass. This Jake fella isn't going to hurt you. I promise."

His reassurances did nothing, however, to stop the flow of Trudy's tears.

"Don't worry," he repeated. "You an' me, we're gonna think of something, but I'm promising you, that Jake son of a bitch ain't gonna hurt you. Not ever again."

Longarm pulled Trudy into his lap and rocked her as if she were a child who needed comforting.

Chapter 37

"Let me ask you something," Longarm said after Trudy's tears slowed to a trickle. "Why don't you just leave this place? I know it's the nicest in town, but that is no advantage if they won't protect you from bein' beat on."

The girl lay in his lap with her face pressed against his belly and her hair tickling his dick. She looked up at him and more tears welled up in her eyes. "I can't," she whispered. "I would love to leave here, but I can't."

Longarm stroked her cheek and smoothed away an errant strand of hair. "Why?" he asked.

"Why can't I leave? I owe the owner. For my train ticket out here from back East. It was . . . it was supposed to be an opportunity for a good job. Not this." She sighed. "Oh, don't get me wrong. It isn't always bad."

Trudy smiled up at him and rolled her head to the side so she could lightly kiss his stomach. "I like being with you, for instance. But there are other times not so good.

You know what I mean? And if I try to leave, the boss will call the sheriff on me and I'll be sent to jail. He told me so."

"Bullshit!" Longarm said.

Trudy wriggled around until she could sit up. "Why did you say that?"

"Because that's what you've been fed, little darlin'. They've fed you a bunch o' bullshit so's to keep you in line. Tell me something, though. Do you really want to leave?"

"Yes," Trudy said vehemently. "Not that I have anyplace else to go, but yes. I really do want out of here."

"Then leave you shall. And no one is gonna come after you for it."

"But how . . ."

"Little darlin', you are going out with me. This morning. Now go grab anything you want t' take with you because you an' me an' my prisoner are walking out of here in about one hour from now. We got us a stagecoach t' catch."

"Can I ask you something?" Trudy said.

"Sure."

"Where are we going?"

Longarm kissed her and began to laugh.

Chapter 38

"Trudy, where do you think you're going?" the madam asked when Longarm, Trudy, and a very relaxed and happy Brian Henry headed for the front door.

The trio stopped and Longarm pulled out his wallet and flipped it open to display his badge. "Deputy U.S. marshal," he said. "These two are my prisoners. They're both goin' with me."

"Balderdash," the madam said. "I know for a fact that this man has been out of your control for a day and a half, and the girl belongs to me."

"The man is indeed my prisoner," Longarm said. "He gave me his parole so he could get laid here. As for the girl, I need her t' testify down in Denver. I'll turn her loose t' come back up here when I'm done with her."

"Testify about what?" the madam demanded.

"That, ma'am, is none o' your affair, but if I need for you t' testify, too, I'll send someone after you. If you don't want t' come, you'll be hauled off in chains so as t' be available when the bailiff calls you."

The woman blinked and visibly tensed. "You wouldn't," she said.

"Try me," Longarm told her.

"I, uh . . ."

"It will take a couple days t' get down to Denver. Then there'll be a couple more for the lawyers t' take depositions. Then we'll see about whether she's needed at the trial, assuming this thing goes to trial," Longarm said. "Don't look for the girl t' be back up here inside o' two weeks, and that's if things go smooth. Could take longer."

"But you will bring her back?"

"More likely, the marshal will give her a pass for the train an' the coaches and give her a meal allowance in cash. But that ain't up to me. I'm only a deputy," he said.

The three of them walked out into the cool of the early morning, leaving the madam behind shaking her head.

When they were well clear of the whorehouse, Brian looked at Trudy, then at Longarm. "Would one of you please tell me what is going on here?"

Both Trudy and Longarm broke into laughter.

Chapter 39

The Gunnison Line coach deposited them in Tincup in the early afternoon, changed horses, and took on two passengers then pulled out almost immediately for Pitkin, Gunnison, and points west.

Longarm, Brian, and Trudy were left standing outside the stage stop with their bags and nowhere to go for another sixteen hours or so until the coach down to Buena Vista left the following morning.

"I wish there was a better hotel hereabouts than I had coming up," Longarm said. "It was pretty rough."

Brian said, "Why not do here what we did in Wyskopf?"

Longarm grinned. "Damn, Brian. An' here I had got to thinking you was just a pretty face. That's a good idea. You two wait here. I'm gonna walk across the street to that saloon an' see what they know about a good whorehouse in town." He looked around. "Well, such as passes for a town up here anyhow. Watch my bag, would you, please?"

He left the two of them waiting while he sidled up to the

bar and paid for a beer and a shot. He dropped the shot into the beer and took a healthy pull at the tin mug—what else in a town called Tincup—then asked the barman, "Where can a man find a really good piece of ass in this burg?"

"I got a couple women. You can use one of them if you like. Dollar for Jennalee, fifty cents for old Hester there," the man said.

Longarm shook his head. "No, what I'm wantin' is a proper place with beds an' such."

The bartender shrugged, apparently not too distressed to be missing out on a cut from one of the whores. "There is a place," he said and proceeded to give directions to it. "If you'd be so kind, tell Michaela that Jonah sent you."

"I'll tell her," Longarm said. He finished his beer and left, heading back across the street to Brian and Trudy.

"I will have to say," Trudy told him when he reached them, "that you're the first lawman I ever saw who leaves his prisoners to run loose like you do."

Longarm grinned. "Brian and me, we have us a agreement."

"You must have."

"Come along, boys and girls. I know where we're going to spend tonight. Uh, I hope."

Chapter 40

"You, you son of a bitch." The roar came out of nowhere. Longarm turned to see the big fellow with the black beard that he'd silenced in the hotel hallway on his way up.

That would have been fine except this time he was holding a rifle. And he looked like he had every intention of using it.

Jesse, Longarm seemed to recall his name as being. Jesse raised the rifle and took aim.

Longarm dove, sweeping both Brian and Trudy off their feet. He landed on top of Brian, driving the breath from the smaller man. Under the circumstances, he was just as happy *not* to be lying on top of Trudy at the moment . . .

Jesse's bullet crackled through the thin mountain air somewhere overhead.

Longarm rolled to the side, his Colt already in hand, and took aim. The .45 belched lead and flame and several dozen paces distant Jesse howled in pain.

The big man, who seemed not to be drunk this time,

hopped on one foot, the other leg bleeding from Longarm's bullet. Even so, he was not ready to give up the fight. He levered another cartridge into place and tried again.

This time it was Brian Henry who screamed in pain.

"Damn you." Longarm shot the man again, this time in the other leg. "Damn you." He fired a third time, his bullet cutting a furrow down Jesse's forearm.

Jesse dropped his rifle.

"Take care o' Brian," Longarm snapped to Trudy as he picked himself up and dashed across the street at Jesse. He wanted to get to the man before he could pick up that rifle and try yet again.

Longarm and Jesse reached the weapon at just about the same time. Longarm yanked on the barrel, twisting it out of Jesse's hand before the man could do any more damage.

"You bastard," Jesse snarled. "You don't fight fair."

"I fight to win," Longarm returned, cranking the lever on Jesse's rifle to eject all the cartridges. "This ain't no boxing match, mister. When I fight, folks tend t' get themselves dead. Consider yourself lucky that I haven't killed you. Yet. Now shut your mouth or you'll find yourself wearing handcuffs an' seeing the world from behind bars."

"You're the fucking law?"

"I am." Longarm tossed the empty rifle into the trash in a nearby alley and took a moment to stare down at the twice-conquered Jesse. "Now shut up. I got things t' do and you ain't one o' them."

He turned and went back across the street to check on Brian and Trudy.

Chapter 41

Brian was sitting up on the edge of a boardwalk in front of a hardware store. Trudy knelt beside him. She had produced a cloth from somewhere and was using it to bandage Brian's upper arm.

"Are you all right, kid?" Longarm asked.

Brian nodded. "I don't think there is any serious damage. It hurts like hell, though." He grinned. "And it startled me something awful, I can tell you that. I'm beginning to think it isn't safe to be around you, Marshal."

"Sometimes I wonder about that myself," Longarm said. He slipped his Colt out of the leather and, first glancing across the street to where Jesse was sitting propped up against the side of a building, proceeded to reload.

"Do you have everything under control here, Trudy?" he asked.

"I think so. The bleeding has stopped now, but I'd like to get a proper bandage for it."

"Give me a minute an' we'll do that," Longarm said. He

walked back across the street and, pointing to the wounded leg, asked Jesse, "Do you need a sawbones for that?"

"Damn right I do."

"We'll get you one. Soon as I get you behind bars."

Jesse roared again. "Jail? What the fuck do you want to send me to jail for? I got a claim to work. If you send me to fucking jail, somebody's apt to come along and jump it."

"Then you shouldn't go around trying to kill people, asshole."

"When I get well again—"

"When you get well again," Longarm said, "you would be well advised to stay clear of me, mister. Next time I'll just go ahead and put a bullet through that thick head of yours. Now where can I find the town marshal up here?"

"Go to hell," Jesse snarled.

"Maybe but not quite yet, no thanks to you," Longarm said.

He motioned to one of the boys who had come to look at the blood now that the shooting was over and told the kid, "If you want t' earn yourself a nickel, go get your town marshal an' bring him here."

The boy took off like a scalded pup and was back two minutes later accompanied by a tall, skinny man who had a badge prominently displayed on his vest.

"Trouble, mister?"

"Not now there isn't." Longarm fished some coins out of his pocket. He did not have a nickel among them so gave the boy a dime for the errand. The kid did not object.

Longarm introduced himself to Tincup town deputy, Harold Moore, and explained the situation. "Assault on a Federal officer. Attempted murder. Discharge of a firearm on a public street. You can prob'ly come up with some other charges if you put your mind to it. For now what I'd like you t' do is to lock this poor, dumb son of a bitch in your jail. Then after you've done that, you might think about getting a doctor t' take a look at that hole in his leg. But first put 'im on the inside looking out. Can you do that for me?"

Moore said, "Sure, but you will have to testify when he comes to trial."

"But you can hold him in jail until then?"

"I can do that for you, Marshal, sure," Moore said.

"When do you think that will be?"

"There's a circuit judge who comes through once a month. He's due back in a little more than two weeks," the local lawman said.

Longarm looked down at Jesse, who was still on the ground. Two weeks behind bars might do the man some good. Or might teach him nothing at all. Either way, it was something. Longarm had no intention whatsoever of coming back up to Tincup for the trial. That would mean Jesse would go free for lack of any testimony against him, but two weeks were better than nothing.

"All right," Longarm said. "Put him on the docket for the next time your judge comes through. In the meantime he can sit his ass in jail an' think about what got him there."

"Whatever you say, Marshal," Moore told him.

"For now, he's yours," Longarm said.

He went back across the street to Brian and Trudy. "Where were we when we were interrupted there? Oh, yeah. Now I remember."

He helped Brian back onto his feet. Trudy jumped up and brushed herself off.

"Let's go find that whorehouse the fella in the saloon

told me about," Longarm said. "We need rooms for tonight an' something to eat."

"When we get there," Brian said with a sheepish grin, "can I . . . I mean, will you . . ."

Longarm laughed. "Yes, Brian, I have enough left over from my poker winnings t' stake you to another girl for tonight."

Chapter 42

Brian Henry grinned, but the flesh of his face and neck were turning ghostly pale. Then he passed out, falling back in Trudy's arms, completely out cold.

Brian's entire side was soaked with blood.

"I thought I had that stopped," Trudy said, sounding worried.

"Shit!" Longarm grumbled. He bent and picked Brian up, cradling the man in his arms like a child. A rather heavy child, though. "We got t' find a doctor," he said. "Fast."

Longarm hustled across the street to where Moore was bending over Jesse. "A doctor, Deputy. We need a doctor for this man. He's been shot."

"Doc Cooper is already on his way," Moore said. "I sent for him to take care of Jesse here."

Longarm heard footsteps approaching, ringing hollow on the boards of the sidewalk, and turned to see a young man carrying a black satchel, surrounded by a flock of young boys drawn to the excitement of it all.

"Are you the doctor?" Longarm asked as the man and his entourage arrived.

"Yes, sir. Is this the patient?"

"They both are," Longarm said, "but that one"—he nodded toward Jesse—"can wait 'til you've seen this one." He was still holding Brian in his arms. Trudy was beside them trying to rouse Brian, who was still out cold.

Cooper moved close and quickly examined Brian. "You tried to stanch the bleeding?"

"I did," Trudy said.

"At first glance I would say that an artery has been clipped by the bullet," Cooper said. "I need to tie it off or he will bleed to death. Get him to my office."

"Where—"

"Follow me." The doctor took off at a swift lope, swift enough that Longarm had difficulty keeping up with him.

Cooper led them to a cabin a block off Tincup's main street. "In here," he said.

He directed Longarm, with Trudy still following, into a back room that he called his surgery. A tall, narrow table lay beneath a bank of hanging lamps.

"Place him there, please. Do you have matches?"

"Pardon me?"

"Matches. You know. For fire?"

"Yes, of course."

"Light all those lamps, please. I want to be able to see what I am doing."

While Longarm was busy with the lamps, Cooper washed his hands with carbolic acid, then said, "You two should leave the room now, please."

Longarm's eyebrow went up. Cooper smiled and said,

"It's all right. I will take the best care of him that I possibly can."

Trudy tugged Longarm's sleeve and pulled him toward the door and the waiting room beyond.

Cooper closed the door behind them.

Chapter 43

It was nearly two hours before the door was opened again and Dr. Cooper came out, his shirtsleeves rolled up and his shirt collar limp.

"Well?" Longarm and Trudy said in unison. "How is he?" Longarm added to that,

Cooper wiped his hands on a small towel and shrugged. "I really don't know yet. Your friend lost a great deal of blood, and it is entirely possible that there could be complications from my corrective surgery. I did get the vessels tied off successfully so the bleeding has stopped, but . . . it is just too soon to tell you anything definite. I will keep him here overnight. Perhaps I can tell you something tomorrow."

"Will he be laid up long?" Longarm asked. He was thinking about their transportation down to Denver for Brian's trial.

"Sir, I don't even know if the man will survive. I certainly can't tell you how long he will be incapacitated," Cooper said.

"All right. We'll come back in the morning," Longarm said. "Maybe you can tell us more then."

On their way out of Cooper's office, Trudy looked up at Longarm and said, "I know you're worried about your friend, but personally I'm hungry. I'll bet you are, too. And we still need to find a room for tonight."

Longarm rubbed the nape of his neck and arched his back. "Yeah," he said. "Yeah, we need t' take care of business." He felt tired all of a sudden.

They found a café and had a quick supper, then walked on to the whorehouse, where they had been heading that afternoon when Jesse disrupted what should have been a pleasant evening and a quick return to Denver.

"All night?" the madam asked.

"Tonight," Longarm said, "an' maybe longer." He explained the situation with Brian.

"And you say you are a deputy United States marshal?" the woman asked. She was thick-bodied, with thinning hair done up in a bun and a sequined dress that fit her poorly.

"Yes, ma'am. This is official business, so the government will pay for our lodging. I got a voucher I can sign over to you for the charges," Longarm said.

The woman eyed Trudy with suspicion. "What about her?"

"She's in my custody," Longarm said. Which was not exactly a lie, depending on how one looked at it. Not exactly the truth either, of course.

"Will you be wanting one of my girls, too?" the madam asked.

"No, ma'am. We won't be having no threesomes at Uncle Sam's expense."

"Well, I do have two spare rooms."

"We won't be needin' but one."

The woman sniffed, although whether that indicated disapproval or simply meant that she had a cold, Longarm did not know.

"All right. Come in. Lila, show these guests to number two, please."

"Yes'm."

Chapter 44

Longarm woke up with a hard-on. It took him a moment to discover why. Trudy had his dick in her mouth and was happily sucking on it.

He smiled and reached down to stroke the back of her head while she continued to suck.

On a whim he pulled her hips around to position her on top of him with her pussy lying above his nose.

Trudy parted her legs to make way for his tongue.

Longarm licked her clitoris while Trudy sucked him. Within seconds she was pumping her hips in time with the touch of his tongue, writhing and quivering. Very quickly she reached a climax, but Longarm continued to lick.

Meanwhile Trudy was sucking hard. She took his dick deep into her mouth and beyond, into her throat and windpipe. Longarm did not know how the girl could breathe like that. But he was awfully pleased with her abilities.

Trudy cupped his balls and tickled them while she

sucked. Every once in a while she would run a fingertip around and around his asshole or dip into it an inch or so.

Longarm felt his cum gather and, despite his best efforts to hold back, burst out into Trudy's hot and eager mouth.

He shuddered. Gave her pussy a friendly kiss and with a sigh rolled the girl off him.

"Lovely way t' wake up," he ventured. "What d'you say we go back to sleep an' try it again the next time we wake up."

Trudy laughed and kissed his cock then swiveled around so they were again lying head to head. "Oh, Custis, I do like you."

"Hush, woman. Go back to sleep." But he was smiling when he said it.

Chapter 45

Longarm and Trudy slept late the following morning. At least Longarm considered it to be late; the sun was up. He sat up on the side of the bed for a minute and rubbed his eyes. Behind him he heard a pleasant voice say, "Good morning, Custis."

He turned and kissed her. "Good morning, Trudy."

"How about some breakfast? If you want to fuck, that's all right, but I'm hungry."

"So am I," he said. He slapped her bare butt and said, "We can fuck later. Chow now."

Trudy bounded from the bed and began pulling on clothes. She was dressed well before he was.

Longarm was about to say something when they heard a knock. He slid his .45 into his hand just in case and went to see who was there. He stood to the side so if someone shot through the closed door, they would miss.

"Yes?"

"Good morning." He was fairly sure the voice was that

of the madam, Mrs. Bell. At least it was definitely a woman's voice. Even so, he was cautious when he opened the door a few inches and peered out.

"Good morning," Mrs. Bell repeated. She was smiling. "I thought I heard voices in there. You're welcome to join us for breakfast. We have plenty."

Longarm returned his Colt to the leather and said, "That's nice o' you, ma'am. We'll be right down, thanks." To Trudy he said, "Are you ready? I just need t' pull my boots on."

He finished dressing then picked up his hat.

"Why are you taking that with you?" Trudy asked.

"'Cause after we eat, I'm goin' over to the doctor's office an' see how Brian is this morning." With a sigh Longarm added, "If he made it through the night. I'm hoping he's on the mend."

"All right, I'll get my bag."

They went downstairs and followed the smell of cooking bacon to the kitchen at the back of the house, where a burly Negro cook was busy laying out bacon, eggs, porridge, and coffee for Mrs. Bell and four working girls.

The madam introduced the four as Pansy, Lila, Little Bit, and Bertha. "Dig in, folks. It's on the house." She smiled. "Tom always cooks for an army. He seems to forget there are so few of us now. And he insists on making this breakfast even though for the girls it is properly supper. They've been working all night. Now they'll go to bed and get some sleep before the gentlemen start coming again."

"You mind yo' trade. I take care o' mine," the cook said, waving a ladle for the porridge. He emphasized his comment by plunging the ladle into the huge bowl of rolled oats and raisins.

"Sit there," Mrs. Bell said, pointing to the place of honor at the head of the table. "And would you care to say grace over our meal, Marshal Long?"

Longarm was taken aback by that request but he did manage to stammer his way through a quick prayer spoken aloud while Trudy and the working girls bowed their heads and clasped their hands.

He hoped that was an omen for a good day to come.

Chapter 46

"Thank you, Mrs. Bell. That was fine." Longarm folded his napkin and laid it beside his plate. "Are you coming, Trudy?" She had been talking with one of the girls—Little Bit? He could not remember which one the dark-haired girl was—throughout the meal. Now Trudy looked up and shook her head.

"Would you mind if I stay here and visit awhile?"

"No, go right ahead." He picked up his Stetson and touched the brim toward the women then left.

The morning was clear and bright. It would have been a near perfect day if he did not have worries on his mind, worries about Brian Henry and whether he had made it through the night after that massive loss of blood followed by the shock of the surgery.

Longarm walked briskly to Dr. Cooper's office. When he went inside, he was confronted by a young man he had not seen before.

"Is, uh, is the doctor in?"

"He's resting. He was up most of the night trying to save a patient."

"Did he?"

"Did he what?"

"Did he save the patient?" Longarm asked.

"Unfortunately the man died," the assistant said.

"Aw, shit," Longarm mumbled. He felt deflated. The beauty of the morning had fled.

"May I ask your name, sir, and your business with the doctor?"

Longarm told him. "The fella that died was my prisoner. I was responsible for him. Responsible for him getting shot, too, dammit."

The young man gave Longarm an odd look. "Charlie was your prisoner? Why? What could that old man have done to bring the law down on him?"

"Charlie? Who the hell are we talkin' about?" Longarm asked.

"Charlie Waters. He's the patient doc lost last night. Of course, Charlie was more than eighty years old. Even so, Doc hated to lose him. He tried everything he knew but he just couldn't save the old man."

"But . . . I thought we was talking about Brian Henry. Young fellow. Doc worked on his arm yesterday."

The assistant smiled. "Oh, him. He's still alive. It looks like he should make it all right. I think he's asleep now, but you can go in if you like. Just don't wake him."

"And if he's awake?" Longarm asked.

"You can talk to him. There's nothing wrong with his voice."

"You had me confused for a minute there," Longarm said.

The assistant smiled again. "You aren't the only one. Go on in."

Chapter 47

"You look all bright eyed and bushy tailed," Longarm said.

"Bright eyed maybe, but hungry," Brian said. "And it tastes like somebody crapped in my mouth."

"I'll see about getting you something t' eat," Longarm told him. "Other than that, how do you feel?"

Brian shrugged, then winced in pain from that slight movement.

Longarm patted his other shoulder and said, "Obviously you ain't exactly in shape t' be jostled around in a stagecoach. We'd best give you a day or two t' heal a little before we head down the mountain to Denver."

"I'm sorry," Brian said. "I don't mean to hold you up." He laughed and added, "Of course, if you need to get back to the city for anything, you could just leave me here. I'm sure I could think of someplace to go."

"Are you changing your mind about going down to face the music?" Longarm asked.

Brian shook his head. "No, not really. I just . . . sometimes

I get to thinking about it, prison and everything, and I get scared."

Longarm pulled out a cheroot, bit the twist off, and lit the slender cigar. He shook his match out and puffed on his smoke for a moment before he said, "It's good for you t' be scared. Means you're thinking. Thinking is good. It'll serve you well inside those walls. If it helps . . . an' I think it will . . . I'll put a word in with the warden. I assume they'll send you down to Canon City. I know the man in charge there. Better yet, if I pull a few strings, maybe I can get the judge to let you do your time right there in the county. I know I can get you taken good care of there."

"You'd do that for me?"

"Of course." Longarm smiled. "Hell, we're friends, aren't we?"

Brian's worried expression turned into a grin. "Yes, sir, I guess we are."

"All right then. Lay back an' rest. I'll see about scaring you up something t' eat, maybe a little nip of somethin' to drink, too. An' don't you worry. I won't let anything bad happen to you. Uh, nothing more, that is. I've already let you be wrecked an' dropped down the side of a mountain an' shot an' near killed."

"I'll forgive you if you can get me a pork chop, Marshal, and somebody to cut it up for me. If you can do that, I think I'll be just fine," Brian said.

Half an hour later Longarm was back carrying a basket covered with a red-and-white-checked napkin.

"Far as I can tell, kid, there ain't a pork chop within fifty miles o' Tincup. But I brought you a nice chunk o' roasted bear meat. It tastes almost like pork. Now let me set you up. I've already cut the meat up for you."

Chapter 48

Longarm collected Trudy from Mrs. Bell's whorehouse and squired her around Tincup—such as there was of it. As a town, Tincup lacked the finer amenities but made up for that with vigor.

The place was little more than a camp, raw and sprawling but full of life. There was something about Tincup that Longarm just plain liked.

The mines in the district were nearly as spread out as the town was, with diggings here, there, and everywhere, small dark holes in the earth that yielded yellow metal.

There was no lack of rough saloons—and a few that approached elegance—plus a scattering of businesses that catered to the needs or the desires of the men who came to burrow in the earth.

"I like it here," Trudy told him over drinks at the Yellow Dog Saloon.

"So do I, but I like Denver just fine, too. Ever been to Denver?" he asked.

Trudy shook her head. "I came up from Santa Fe. I've never seen Denver."

"It's quite the city," Longarm said. He stood and stretched. "Can I get you another beer?"

"No, thanks. I'm not finished with this one."

"Excuse me then. I'll be right back." He went to the bar and got himself another beer and a shot and carried them back to the table, where a rough-looking miner was trying to talk Trudy into going with him.

The fellow thought about challenging Longarm, who could see the hostility in the man's eyes and in his posture. He tensed for a moment, then relaxed and turned away from the table.

Longarm sat. He smiled. "You're popular with the fellows. Are you sure you don't want anything?"

"I do want something," Trudy said. "I want to talk with you."

"All right, kid. I'm listening."

"While you were away this morning, I was talking with Little Bit and the other girls. They tell me that Mrs. Bell is a wonderful madam. For one thing, she owns the house herself. She isn't working for some bastard slave driver. She's good to her girls. Pays well. Treats the girls right. She protects them from gentlemen callers who want more than a girl is willing to give."

Longarm nodded and lit another cheroot. "Are you tryin' to tell me something?"

"Yes, I am. I . . . I'm grateful to you for getting me out of a bad situation back there in Wyskopf. I appreciate it. I always will. And if you want me, like for a mistress or something, I will go with you."

"But . . ."

"But Mrs. Bell is short on girls and . . . well, I'd like to work in her house." Trudy sat back with a grimace. "There. I said it. Are you mad at me?"

Longarm laughed and leaned forward. He kissed her on the forehead and said, "Then may I have the honor of bein' your first customer in Miz Bell's house?"

"You aren't mad? Really?"

"Really," he assured her. "If that's what you want, then that's what I want for you."

"Thank you, Custis. Thank you. I was worried that . . . well, I was just worried, that's all. Thank you."

"Let's go do some shopping," he said. "I want t' buy you something to remember me by. What would you like? Something t' start your new life with, maybe."

"I don't know but it has been ever so long since I've been able to shop and just look at everything. Can we do that? Really?"

"Really," he told her.

Trudy jumped up so quickly she nearly tipped her chair over.

"Hold on," Longarm said. He downed his shot and drained off his beer. He was going to need some fortification, he thought, if he was going to be dragged through Tincup's stores in search of Trudy's keepsake.

"All right," he said. "Let's go."

Chapter 49

"Oh, Custis, look!"

Longarm paid no attention, thinking Trudy was just pointing out some geegaw or trifle. Which she had been doing ever since they set out on her shopping excursion.

She tugged at Longarm's sleeve and pointed down the street. "I think that lady is in trouble, Custis."

He looked then and did not like what he saw. A man, one of the roughly dressed miners so often seen on the streets of Tincup, was saying something to a lady who was caught in the middle of the street. She kept turning away from him while he kept on barking into her face.

They were too far away for Longarm to hear what was being said, but it was obvious from the posture of both that the man was pressing unwanted advances on the woman.

The lady was dressed in plain but decent clothes. Longarm could not see her expression because of a deeply hooded bonnet she wore. It, too, was plain but decent, made of the same material as her dress.

"He tried to touch her, Custis. Did you see?"

"Yeah, damn him. I saw," Longarm said, scowling.

Longarm himself was something of a rake and knew a bit about the ways to approach a woman, respectable or otherwise. But he did not countenance unwelcome advances.

"Wait here," he said, flinging the stub of his cheroot into the street and taking long, determined strides toward the couple.

When he got close enough to overhear what was going on with the two, he heard the man say something about a "stuck-up bitch," obviously accusing the lady.

That was bad enough, but the man took hold of the woman and tried to force a kiss on her.

Instead of screaming for help, the lady tried to pull away. The man was too strong for her to resist. He had one hand on her arm and was grabbing for her breast with his free hand.

That was too much for Longarm.

He reached the two and without slowing put his full strength plus the impetus of his charging body into a crushing blow to the shelf of the man's jaw.

The fellow's head snapped back and his eyes rolled upward until only the whites showed. He was sent flying onto the ground, out cold from the powerful force of Longarm's blow.

"Sorry, miss," Longarm said. He shook his hand. It stung. He hoped he had not broken a bone in it.

He turned and looked beneath the deep brim of her bonnet . . . and his heart felt like it skipped a beat.

She was . . . she was beautiful. No, more than beautiful. She was like a porcelain doll. Exquisite. Heart-shaped face. Long eyelashes. Soft, full lips. Bright, huge eyes. Green, he thought, although her face was so deeply shaded by the bonnet that he could not be sure about that.

She was young but no child. Somewhere in her twenties or very early thirties, he judged.

And she was the loveliest woman he . . .

"Custis? Is everything all right, Custis?" Trudy had come along behind him. Now she moved to his side and hooked her arm into his.

"Yes, uh . . . yes," he said. To the lady he touched the brim of his Stetson and made a little half bow. "My apologies, miss. I hope you're all right."

"I am fine, thank you." Her voice was low and, he thought, quite beautiful.

The man who had been bothering her scrambled to his feet, thought about objecting to his treatment, but after one look at Longarm, just turned and slunk away.

"If there is anything . . ." Longarm did not know how to finish the sentence.

Besides, he was there on business. His job was to deliver Brian Henry down to the court in Denver. He really should keep that in mind.

He bobbed his head toward the lady again and turned away, taking Trudy with him, resuming their search for the perfect gift he might give her.

Chapter 50

"You're wonderful, Custis. Thank you for everything you have done for me," Trudy said, rising on tiptoes to kiss him. "Thank you."

"You're a good girl, Trudy. I have t' admit I'll miss you. We been together, what, six days? I've enjoyed every moment of it." He laughed. "Especially since you're such a good fuck."

He gave her a gentle kiss and said, "If Mrs. Bell doesn't treat you right, come down to Denver. The U.S. Marshal's Office will know where t' find me."

"I will. I promise," Trudy said.

"G'bye now, lass." He kissed her one last time and as a tease reached around and gave her ass a squeeze. Trudy squealed and rose onto her toes again.

Longarm touched the brim of his Stetson to her, then turned away. He still needed to collect Brian from the doctor's office, and the stagecoach would not wait for them.

Brian Henry was ready when Longarm got there.

Longarm had already given the doctor a voucher to pay for Brian's care.

Brian eyed a light, muslin poke that Longarm was carrying in addition to his carpetbag. "What do you have there, Marshal?"

"Breakfast," Longarm said. "I liberated some biscuits from Mrs. Bell's table. We can eat them along the way. Don't want t' be late, though. I already wired my office to expect us. An' why the delay of so long."

The two men walked together to the stage stop. They had to wait only a matter of minutes until the coach pulled to a rocking halt beside the boardwalk.

By then, five other passengers had arrived ready to travel down to the railroad deep in the Arkansas River Valley. One of them was a lady. She was wearing a bonnet and not standing close to the others. Longarm could not see her face, but her figure was trim, her bust perky, and her waist almost impossibly small.

Longarm thought . . . He smiled. It was the same beautiful young woman he had seen on the street some days earlier. When she turned in his direction, he smiled and doffed his hat.

The girl returned the smile, and once again his heart did cartwheels inside his chest.

This, he thought, was going to be a very pleasant ride down the mountain.

Chapter 51

"Why are we stopping, driver?" one of the passengers called up to the driving box.

"Got to ford a stream. Damn ford is full of rocks. I don't want one of my horses breaking a leg, so we got to take it slow. You folks just set easy down there. Me and my horses know what we're doing."

Brian Henry and several of the other passengers appeared to be dozing. Longarm pretended to. It was a pretext, though. It allowed him to peer out from beneath the brim of his hat and stare at the lady without being rude about it. Lordy, she was the prettiest thing he believed he had ever seen. *Ever!*

He wondered what her name was. Wondered what business was taking her down to the railroad. If indeed that was where she was headed. Wondered, too, if she was married. It would be one lucky son of a bitch who married her.

He heard the approach of hoofbeats. The coach came to a complete standstill.

"All right, pops. You know what we want." It was a man's voice.

Longarm opened his eyes and sat forward on his seat bench. He did not like the sound of that voice. There was something about it . . .

"Throw it down, pops." A different voice, higher pitched but also a man's.

Longarm's .45 slid into his hand and he looked out. He turned his head and to the other passengers said, "Get down as low as you can. There's gonna be shooting here."

He knelt at the side window and raised his .45.

He heard something hollow inside his skull and felt a dull pain in the back of his head.

Blackness descended over him and Longarm knew nothing else.

Chapter 52

"Marshal. Marshal Long. Wake up, sir."

Longarm opened his eyes. His head hurt something fierce and he felt like he wanted to throw up. Brian Henry was squatting over him, a worried look on his face.

"Wake up, sir."

Longarm blinked and Brian tugged at his arm, pulling him into a sitting position. He was on the ground, he discovered, in the shade of the stagecoach. Brian, or someone, must have dragged him out of the coach and laid him out beside it.

"I'm . . . all right," he croaked. That was a lie but at least it was an optimistic one. "What's happened?"

"Highwaymen, Marshal. Robbers. There was a strongbox going down to the railroad. They took it. They kidnapped that lady, too," Brian told him.

"How'd I end up down here?"

"One of the passengers, Marshal. He wasn't a passenger after all. He must have been in league with the bandits.

You looked out the window, and while your back was turned, he whacked you with the butt of his pistol. I guess your hat saved you from having your head split wide open."

"How long . . . have I been out?"

"I don't know, sir. A half hour maybe."

"The driver and other passengers?"

"The driver is dead. He wouldn't give them the box so they shot him. The other passengers took off back to Tincup."

"And the lady?"

Brian shook his head. "They took her with them. I won't repeat the things they said they were going to do to her, but it isn't good."

Longarm grunted. "Help me stand up, will you?"

Brian hauled Longarm upright. Longarm felt of his pockets. He had not been robbed, but his Colt was missing.

"Have you seen my gun, Brian? D'you know what's happened to it?"

Brian nodded. "One of the robbers took your pistol. They robbed the other passengers, too."

"Why didn't they rob me, too?"

Brian shrugged. "Maybe they thought you were dead, sir. They didn't rob the driver either except to take the strongbox."

"Ain't this a helluva mess," Longarm said. "And they took the lady? She wasn't with them?"

"Oh, no, sir. She fought them like a wildcat. She scratched and kicked. One of them finally hit her, hit her hard, to make her shut up."

"Well, shit." Longarm walked the few paces to the creek, his legs rubbery, and knelt. Bending low, he immersed his face into the icy stream and held it there for a moment while the cold water revived and refreshed him. He drank, then stood again, feeling much better.

"Where're the horses?" he asked, just then noticing that the coach was standing still with no horses hitched to it.

"The others. They took them," Brian said.

"Shit," Longarm repeated. He climbed onto the driving box of the light coach and examined the body of the dead jehu. The man was not wearing a holster, but he was lying on top of his shotgun, an L.C. Smith double twelve cut down to coach gun length.

Longarm broke the action and looked into the tubes. Both were loaded with buckshot. He checked the driver's pockets and found two more shells for the gun. Those also were loaded with buck.

He dropped the spare shells into his own pocket along with his supply of spare .45 cartridges—useless unless he found another revolver—and climbed back down again, taking the shotgun with him.

"Did you see which way they went?" he asked.

"The robbers, sir, or the other passengers?"

"The robbers. I know where the passengers went. Back to Tincup, didn't you say?"

Brian bobbed his head in agreement. "Hadn't we better start back, too? It will be dark before too long."

Longarm glanced up at the sky, not so much to ascertain the time of day as to give himself a moment to think. When he looked down again, he said, "Okay, here's what we'll do. I want you t' go back to Tincup alone. You can't be chasing after road agents with your arm still not healed. And anyway, it's still my responsibility to get you down to Denver safe for trial." He smiled. "You are still my prisoner, y'know."

"Yes, sir, but—"

"No buts about it. Go back to Tincup. Find Trudy. She'll help you until I get there."

"What about you, Marshal?"

Longarm felt of his vest pocket to make sure his derringer was where it was supposed to be. He hefted the short-barreled shotgun and grinned. Or grimaced. It was hard to tell which the expression was intended to be.

"Me? I'm going after those sons o' bitches that kidnapped the lady."

Chapter 53

There was one good thing about walking. It was slower and closer to the ground than being on horseback would have been and that made it easier to track.

The bad thing was that, well, he was walking.

Longarm used up the last of the daylight following the horses, three of them. When it became too dark to be sure of the tracking, he had no choice but to stop for the night.

The stagecoach robbers were at least an hour ahead of him and anyway knew where they were going. It would not be necessary for them to stop just because night fell.

It occurred to Longarm that he was assuming the gang was staying somewhere close. It was also possible they could have been passing through and their destination was hundreds of miles away. Still, the odds were that they were fairly local and would take their loot and head for home.

If they'd intended to travel far, he reasoned, they would have stayed at the robbery site long enough to break open the strongbox and transfer its contents to their saddles. As it was, they took the box with them to be opened later. That implied they did not intend to travel far.

But how far, dammit? And where?

He had no choice but to stop for the night even though that meant the lady would spend at least one night as the plaything of the robbers.

Longarm hated to think what they might be doing to her, but he could do nothing to help her unless he could find her, and he could not find her unless there was enough light to let him follow the tracks.

Tracking was hard enough in the mountains anyway since it was over more rock and gravel than soft soil.

When darkness brought him to a halt and he was no longer warmed by exercise, he felt the gathering cold of the high country air.

He collected some fallen wood and pinecones and made a fire. That helped some, enough to allow him to fall asleep. Later, with the fire burned out and no longer warming him, he woke up shivering and was unable to go back to sleep because of the high mountain cold.

It was not a comfortable night, and come morning, Longarm was in a foul mood. He was dead tired and bleary-eyed from lack of sleep, miserably cold, thirsty, and hungry.

His gut rumbled and his mouth tasted like someone shit in it.

And to top it all off, he was out of cigars.

Pity the poor son of a bitch who got in his way this day.

Chapter 54

He smelled the smoke before he saw anything, put his nose into the breeze, and followed it to a small hollow or cirque tucked into the mountainside.

A log cabin backed up to a rock face and a corral made of aspen rails was lower on the slope, both of those surrounded by more aspen. On a slope below the corral was a stand of lush grass that showed signs of having been harvested for wild hay. At the foot of the cirque a thin creek ran.

Handy, Longarm thought. It formed a near perfect hideout, hard to find and easy to defend.

Easy to defend, he thought with a wry grin, if—big if—the occupants knew there were enemies afoot.

Literally afoot in his case. The fact was that his feet hurt after so much walking on such rocky ground. But he was here now, and he was fairly certain this was where the robbers had dragged the lady from the stagecoach.

He thought about removing his boots and soaking his feet in the cold water of the stream, but there was too great a possibility that one of the gang might come out for something—to feed the horses or bring in wood for the stove or simply to take a piss—and discover him sitting there making a perfect target of himself.

Better, he decided, to worry about his feet after business was taken care of.

And the law was his business. The law . . . and sometimes death.

Longarm once again checked the loads in the shotgun, pulled back the steel hammers, and soft-footed his way out of the aspens to the cabin.

There were no windows cut into the log walls of the cabin and only one door. The cabin was built tight against the cliff face behind it. That would have made it easier to build. Logs were required for only three sides. But that also meant there was no back way out, no escape in that direction.

Longarm wished for a cheroot, a cigar, even a cigarillo. He had none of those. But he did have matches in his pocket.

He set the shotgun aside for a moment and walked through the aspen grove to a stand of pine beyond where he gathered an armload of dry needles and fallen pinecones. He carried those back to the cabin and crept close to the south-facing log wall, choosing the south face on the assumption that it would have received full sun ever since the cabin was built. That wall was apt to be the driest of the three.

He piled the load of needles against the wall and retrieved the shotgun.

Then he struck a match and applied it to the pile of tinder.

He shifted position a few feet to get a good, close view of the cabin door.

And waited.

Chapter 55

Two men came boiling out of the cabin. They were wearing red flannel longjohns and carried revolvers in their hands. There was fire in their eyes as well as on the cabin wall.

Longarm waited until they were well clear of the doorway then stood and, from a distance of no more than fifteen feet, fired his right barrel at the man on the left and the remaining load at the man on the right.

The heavy load of buckshot cut the men into bloody rags. Both fell without a twitch.

When they were down and obviously dead, Longarm remembered to mutter under his breath, "This is the law. Come out an' surrender."

Immediately Longarm dropped to a knee and thumbed the lever to break the action of the scattergun. Not knowing if there could be any more members of the robber gang inside, he quickly yanked out the empty brass shells and shoved in his last two spares.

"This is Deputy United States Marshal Custis Long,"

he called out, this time in a loud voice. "You're surrounded. Come out with your hands up. No guns."

He figured he had anyone inside the cabin as good as surrounded so it was not completely a lie.

He held the shotgun at the ready. For half a minute or so there was no movement from within the cabin. Then the lady from the stagecoach appeared at the doorway.

"Don't shoot," she called. "There's just me here. Are you . . . are you really a deputy?"

Longarm stood and let the hammers gently down on the shot shells in the double-barrel. He hurried to the woman and swept his hat off. "Are you all right, ma'am?"

Her only answer was to begin crying, her slender frame wracked by spasms of . . . Joy? Fear? Sorrow? Whatever emotion held sway inside her was powerful.

"You're all right now, ma'am." It was probably the wrong thing to say under the circumstances, but he blurted out, "Is that bacon I can smell cookin' in there?"

The lady gave him a disbelieving look, then burst into laughter, the tears forgotten at least for the moment.

"Hey," he said, "I'm sorry, but I ain't had nothing to eat since we left Tincup."

She straightened up and used the back of her hand to scrub the tears from her eyes, then said, "I was cooking dinner for them, but I see they won't be needing it so you might as well have it if you can get it out before the place burns down."

Longarm grinned, his stomach rumbling emptily, and stepped inside the hideout.

Chapter 56

Flames were already eating away at one end of the front wall. Longarm made sure the lady was well clear then grabbed a pair of saddles that were stacked close to the door. He threw those outside then picked up a pot of beans that was sitting on the table and grabbed the skillet of bacon frying on the stove.

He carried everything outside and motioned for the woman to join him. "Hungry?"

"No. Are you really a deputy?"

"Yes, ma'am."

"You were on the stagecoach," she said.

"Yes, ma'am."

"The other man. Did I hear someone say that he was your prisoner?"

"Yes, ma'am." While they chatted, Longarm was busy using his pocket knife to shovel cold beans into his mouth. The bacon would have to wait until it cooled a little as it had been sizzling on the stove.

"Did he escape after they kidnapped me?"

"No, ma'am. He'll meet us in Tincup."

"You gave him parole until then?"

Longarm grinned. "Sort of. Him and me been through quite a bit together. I figure I can trust him, an' if it turns out I'm wrong about that, then, well, I can catch him again."

"You seem very sure of yourself."

"I got reason to be. Mind if I ask something now?" The bacon had cooled enough that he was able to pick up some with his fingers so he set the bean pot down. "There was a third man. The one makin' like he was a passenger. Where'd he get to?"

"He rode into Tincup to mail a ransom note," the woman said.

"They was tryin' to get ransom from your husband?"

"From my father. I'm not married."

"That surprises me. A good-looking woman like you should be married," Longarm said then quickly added, "I'm sorry, miss. It's none o' my business. I shouldn't ought to say such a thing."

"That is quite all right, Marshal. I don't doubt that you saved my life. I certainly owe you straight answers to anything you care to ask." She hesitated then said, "Something that I notice you haven't asked is whether those men molested me."

"That's none o' my business either," he said. "An' it shouldn't matter anyhow. They're dead now. They can't tell no tales, and it's no one else's business what you mighta had t' do to survive with them bastards. So I didn't ask that question an' I won't."

"Thank you, Marshal. May I suggest something?"

"O' course," he said.

"May I suggest, under the circumstances, that we introduce ourselves?"

Longarm gaped at her. "We haven't . . . really . . ." Then he began to laugh. The lady chuckled, too.

On the slope above them, the cabin was now fully engulfed in flames.

Chapter 57

"It's my pleasure t' meet you, Julia Branscomb." He smiled. "Even if the circumstances might've been better."

Longarm introduced himself, and Julia extended her hand. She had a forthright manner, and he liked her.

"D'you want some o' this?" he asked, indicating the skillet of bacon.

She shook her head. "It's all yours."

"I'll just grab another bite or two, then we'll saddle those horses an' head for Tincup. It'd be best if we could get there before your father receives that ransom note, lest he go from one end o' Tincup to the next tryin' to borrow money for your freedom. Do you know how they intended t' deliver that note an' get the money?"

"The man was going to mail the note. I think . . . they never came right out and said it, but I think once they had the money, they intended to kill me and go down to Arizona Territory, maybe on south to Mexico."

"Your father would've paid?"

"Yes, he would." There was no doubt in her voice when she said that. The man would have paid. She was certain of it.

"Then we'd better get there first," Longarm said. "How much were they asking for anyhow?"

"Fifteen thousand, they said. Five thousand for each of them."

Longarm whistled softly through his teeth. "That's a heap of money. Do you think he could raise that much?"

"I do," she said.

He grunted and stuffed the last piece of bacon into his mouth. He could feel the intense heat from the burning cabin. "Scuse me," he mumbled around the bacon.

Longarm picked up the saddles and carried them down to the corral, where the horses were becoming nervous and unsettled because of the smoke coming from the cabin.

The two dead men were roughly dressed. He had not seen either of them before. Certainly neither was the faux passenger who'd hit him from behind during the robbery.

The third man had been a passenger inside the coach. Longarm had seen that one before and would recognize him when he found the son of a bitch in Tincup.

And that would be soon. Very soon.

He picked up the revolvers the dead robbers had on them, chose the better of the two, and shoved it into his holster. The single-action Colt was not as fine as his own double-action model, but it would do the job.

He pushed the spare into his waistband.

"May I have that extra pistol, Custis? Would you mind?"

"O' course not." He handed the revolver to Julia, who promptly flicked open the loading gate and spun the cylinder to make sure the gun was loaded. Longarm liked that.

The woman knew how to handle a firearm and was certainly not afraid of them the way some women were or professed to be.

Longarm knelt and removed a handful of cartridges from the belt of one of the dead men. He dropped them into his coat pocket, making sure he had spares if he needed them.

He saddled both horses and led them out of the corral.

"Take your pick," he told Julia.

She chose a short, shaggy little brown, leaving the leggy sorrel for Longarm.

He started toward her to help her onto the saddle, but help was not needed. Julia stepped into the stirrup and swung up onto her horse, sitting it astride with no nonsense about trying to ride sidesaddle. She seemed quite comfortable on the animal.

Longarm stepped onto the sorrel and smiled. He touched the brim of his Stetson and said, "Let's go find that fella before he gives your papa a heart attack from worry."

Chapter 58

It was well past nightfall when they found their way to Tincup after making several false starts along the way.

"What I'm gonna suggest," Longarm said, dismounting in front of one of the saloons, "is that you go home. Assure your dad that you're all right now. Let him see that you're safe. I figure the third robber will be haunting the saloons while he waits for the ransom money t' be paid.

"I'll settle with him first an' see him behind bars, then I'll find you an' let you know that it's over. Is that all right with you?"

Julia nodded. "Do you know where I live?"

"No, of course not," Longarm said.

"You go to the last cross street and turn left. We are the last house on the right."

"All right. Got it. I'll meet you there sometime later, hopefully this evening."

Julia nodded and reined away, prodding the brown into motion.

Longarm watched her go, thoroughly enjoying the view. Miss Julia Branscomb had a very nicely shaped ass.

Ogling the lady did nothing toward ending this, though. He tied the sorrel to a hitching rail and stepped inside the first of Tincup's saloons.

An hour later Longarm spotted a man wearing a corduroy coat with leather sleeve patches and velvet inserts on the collar. He had seen that coat before. On the stagecoach not long before he was knocked out by that blow from behind.

He felt the unfamiliar Colt in his holster, easing it out for a half inch or so then letting it fall back into place, making sure it was free in the leather and would come to hand properly.

Then he stepped forward to brace the son of a bitch who'd robbed and kidnapped and had the very foolish idea that he could get away with his crimes.

Chapter 59

"Hold still. Don't move or I'll blow your head apart." Longarm crowded close behind the man in the corduroy coat and pressed the muzzle of his .45 to the back of the man's head.

"Jesus, mister. I . . . I've only got a few dollars on me," the fellow stammered.

"I'm a Federal deputy marshal, and you are under arrest on charges of robbery and kidnapping," Longarm said.

Kidnapping, he knew, was not a Federal crime. Any charge about that would have to be a matter of state law. But the robbery charge could be made to stick if so much as a postcard was taken; robbery of the mail was indeed a Federal matter, and Longarm was well within his rights to place that charge.

"Do . . . not . . . move," he said, keeping the revolver held tight to the back of the fellow's head and reaching for his handcuffs with his left hand.

"All right now. Very carefully put your hands down behind your back. Good. Now do not move. Not a quiver or you might make my finger move. An' trust me, that would fuck up your whole day, mister. There. That's right. Hold still now."

He snapped the handcuffs in place, then shoved the revolver back into his holster and reached around the man to check him for weapons.

Longarm frowned. The man was not armed. That seemed odd, that a kidnapper would not have a gun on him. Still, it was what it was, and the man chose to walk the streets of Tincup without a weapon on his person.

"All right. Turn around."

"I remember you. You were on that stagecoach," the man said. "Are you really a deputy?"

Longarm nodded.

"The others of us sure as hell thought that fella killed you. He hit you awfully hard."

"Don't try an' wiggle out of this," Longarm said. "I got you dead to rights."

"Deputy, I don't know what you think I've done, but I can't think of any crime I've committed. I'm a mining engineer. I was on my way to Leadville when that coach was held up."

"You hit me in the back of the head," Longarm said.

"Oh, you were hit all right, but not by me. That was the skinny man with the dark hair and handlebar mustache."

"I think you're lying," Longarm said.

"I know how I can prove it," the nicely dressed mining engineer said. "That man that was with you. The little guy. Ask him. He can verify what I'm saying."

"I don't know where Brian is right now."

"I do," the prisoner said. "I can take you there."

Without waiting for Longarm to respond, the man turned, hands locked behind him in the steel cuffs, and headed for the door.

Chapter 60

The fellow led Longarm to Mrs. Bell's whorehouse, not exactly a surprise. Brian had to be somewhere, and Mrs. Bell's was without question the nicest place in Tincup.

There was a wait of only a few seconds after Longarm tugged the bell pull until Mrs. Bell herself opened the door for them.

The lady smiled when she saw them. "Marshal Long. How very nice to see you again. Have you come to see Mr. Henry?" A chuckle joined her smile. "Or are you here to see our Trudy?"

"I'd like t' see Brian if you don't mind. Official business, I'm afraid," Longarm said.

"He thinks I robbed the stagecoach," the engineer put in.

"Oh, Lewis. Surely a nice man like you would never do such a thing," the madam said.

"That's what I've been trying to tell him," Lewis said.

"Well, come in, both of you. Mr. Henry is upstairs. You

boys wait in the parlor. I will tell Mr. Henry he is needed down here."

Longarm prodded Lewis into the parlor. Both sat but Longarm kept his Colt ready.

Two of the girls peeped out from the kitchen to see if their services were needed, but they quickly retreated when they saw Longarm's .45.

It was several minutes before Brian came downstairs. He was barefoot and his hair was disheveled. Trudy was with him. She was wearing only a thin, cotton shift and was also barefoot. It seemed obvious that she was the girl Brian had chosen for the evening.

Longarm was not sure how he felt about that. Trudy was a whore. He understood that, of course. She went with whoever paid for her services. But . . . Brian? After the time the three of them had been together and Trudy was Longarm's? It seemed wrong to him somehow.

He stood when they came into the room.

Trudy came to him and went onto tiptoes to plant a kiss on the side of his jaw. "It's so nice to see you again, Custis."

"Good t' see you, too, darlin', but I need t' see Brian for a minute." He kissed her on her forehead and turned to Brian.

"During that robbery, Brian, did you see this man an' what he was doing?"

"Yes, of course, I remember him. He was one of the passengers."

"He isn't the one that hit me in the back o' the head?"

"No, that man was the skinny fellow with the big mustache and the derby hat."

"That's what I've been trying to tell him, but he didn't believe me," Lewis said.

"Well, shit. Sorry about that," Longarm said. "Turn

around an' I'll unlock those bracelets." To Brian Henry, he said, "D'you have any idea where I can find that fella from the robbery?"

"I think so," Brian said. "If I remember correctly, he's been sitting on the porch outside the home of a man named Branscomb."

"Oh, dear Jesus," Longarm groaned. "An' I sent Julia right to the son of a bitch."

Without a word of explanation, Longarm turned and bolted out of Mrs. Bell's whorehouse.

Chapter 61

They were there, all right. Julia, the skinny kidnapper, and Julia's father, Aaron Branscomb. They were in the parlor, every lamp in the place burning bright, and the kidnapper holding a pistol on the two others.

Longarm did not immediately step up onto the porch, where his boots were likely to make noise on the floorboards. Instead he went around to the side of the house and looked through an open window with thin curtains fluttering lightly in the breeze.

The temptation was strong to simply take careful aim and shoot the skinny son of a bitch who had tried to brain him back there in the stagecoach. Tried his best and apparently thought he had killed Longarm.

It would have been an easy shot to make. The bastard was not twenty feet away. But dammit, his job was not to take revenge on anyone who'd wronged him but to put under arrest anyone who'd wronged the law. That would include this low-life piece of shit.

Longarm went so far as to take that careful aim, lining the sights of the revolver on the head of the kidnapper.

He could not pull the trigger. He was a lawman, a deputy United States marshal, not an assassin, and he could not do it, could not shoot the man down from ambush.

Instead, scowling with pent-up anger, he returned to the front of the little house and stepped up onto the porch, his boots ringing hollow on the boards.

It had to be obvious to anyone inside that someone was coming to the door. Stealth was out of the question now, so the hell with it.

In a loud, harsh voice, Longarm called, "Open up. Deputy U.S. marshal here. You're under arrest."

He snatched the screen door open and turned the knob to release the latch and shove the front door open.

Except . . . the damn door was locked. The knob did not turn under his hand and the latch did not release.

Inside he heard a sudden flurry of motion and a sound like falling bodies.

Julia screamed and a man's voice shouted something Longarm could not make out.

He heard a gunshot. Then another.

Longarm reared back and kicked the door, planting his boot hard just to the side of the latch.

The door flew open and he charged inside.

Chapter 62

Aaron Branscomb was down on the floor. He was leaking blood onto a braided rag rug there. Longarm could not be sure where the aging man's wounds were, but from the amount of cussing Branscomb was giving the kidnapper, he was far from dying.

Longarm admired the depth and variety of the swearing. And in front of Branscomb's daughter, too.

The kidnapper had the muzzle of his revolver pressed into Julia's right ear, and the hammer on the gun was in full cock position. It would take only a slight squeeze of the trigger and Julia Branscomb would die.

"You son of a bitch," the skinny kidnapper snarled. "I thought you was dead."

"You tried hard enough," Longarm said. "Damn near got it done. Now I'm putting you under arrest. You'll stand trial for the murder of that stagecoach driver, robbery, kidnapping, maybe for other stuff, too. There will be time enough to think about all that once you're behind bars, which is where you rightly belong."

"Like hell you're taking me in, lawman. Make one move toward me and this girl is dead."

Longarm's .45 remained steady on the son of a bitch. He reached into his pocket and extracted a cigar, bit the twist from it and spit the tobacco out, dipped into a vest pocket for a match, and struck it. He lit his cigar and blew a stream of smoke, which quickly dissipated.

He grunted and raised his Colt a little. With the cheroot gritted between his teeth, he said, "Then what?"

"Huh?"

"You heard me. You'll shoot the girl, you said. Well, then what? She'll fall down. You won't have no shield no more. An' before you can cock that shooter for another shot, I will 've put a bullet between your eyes, stupid. If she dies, you die. It's that simple. Or if you want to keep on living, you lay your gun down, let her go, an' I put you under arrest. Your choice. But I guaran-damn-tee, if you shoot her, you die. Now what d'you want to do?"

"I . . . I said I'll shoot her," the kidnapper blustered again.

"An' I said what I said. Now make up your mind, but do it quick. That old man there needs t' see a doctor for what you done to him. If you don't decide, I'm gonna go ahead and put a bullet in you anyhow, so you might as well give yourself up to the law now an' save yourself from bein' dead." Longarm blew another stream of white smoke into the air between them.

"Damn you!" the kidnapper cried. He pushed Julia aside and brought the muzzle of his revolver around toward Longarm.

Longarm's Colt roared before the kidnapper could take aim.

And that promise of a bullet between the eyes was fulfilled. The man's head snapped back and the back of his head seemed to explode as Longarm's bullet burst completely through and out the other side. He was dead before his corpse hit the floor.

Chapter 63

"Help me get your father to the doctor, miss."

Julia made no pretenses of girly delicacy. She dropped to her knees and cradled her dad, brushing the hair out of his eyes and crying just a little. Also as quickly as she went down, she hopped up again and took hold of Aaron's lower legs.

"Help me," she appealed, looking up at Longarm with those fantastic eyes.

He scooped up Aaron's upper body and lifted. Fortunately the old man was not very heavy. Between the two of them, they horsed him out the front door and across the porch.

"This isn't gonna work," Longarm said. "Let me get him." He turned Aaron facedown, picked him up, and draped the man's body over his shoulder. "That's better," he grunted when he had the position the way he wanted it. "Come on, girl."

"You could ask me, young man," Aaron said from somewhere behind Longarm's head and just to the side.

"Sorry. I thought you were passed out," Longarm said.

"It will take more than a bullet to do that," Aaron declared. His breathing came in fits and starts, interrupted at times by his abdomen bouncing heavily on Longarm's shoulder. "Are you the young deputy my daughter has been swooning over ever since the moment she got home?"

"Swooning?"

"Yes, swooning."

"I'll be damned," Longarm exclaimed, utterly floored by the idea of Julia Branscomb "swooning" over him.

"Possibly," Aaron said, "but first at least give my daughter a look. It would take a man with strong convictions to hold on to her. She says you are a man . . . ouch . . . a man of action. She admires that. Oh, she is bold at times. But ignore that. She's really a softie inside."

"If you say so." Longarm turned to look. Julia was close behind them and had to have heard every word her father said.

After a block or so, she said, "Do you know where we're going?"

"To the doctor's, of course."

"Do you have any idea where that is?"

"Yes. Do you?"

"Of course."

"Then run on ahead an' tell the man we're on our way." Longarm was beginning to tire and would not have appreciated any delays outside the doctor's door. Besides, he wanted to have a word with Aaron when Julia was not listening.

She gave him a suspicious glance but broke into a most unladylike gallop ahead of them.

"Now," Longarm said to Aaron. "Tell me more about this."

Chapter 64

The two of them, Custis Long and Julia Branscomb, sat in rocking chairs on the doctor's porch, waiting for word about her father.

"Mind if I smoke?" he asked.

"I thought you said you were out of cigars."

"I was. Bought some more. They let you do that in stores, y'know."

"And you, sir, are a smart-ass," Julia said.

"Is that a complaint?"

"Merely an observation."

Longarm took out a cheroot, bit the twist off, and spit it aside. He struck a match and applied it appropriately, sucked in some of the smoke, and slowly let it trickle out again.

"May I?" Julia asked, reaching across the space between their chairs.

"You want t' smoke?"

"Now and then," she said. "Not usually in public, but at this hour, who's to see?"

He handed her the cigar and she did indeed take a puff. She drew the smoke deep, held it in her lungs for a moment, and exhaled. "Not bad," she said.

"Damn good," he countered.

Julia returned the cigar, and Longarm clamped it between his teeth.

They sat in silence for a time, their rocking chairs going back and forth. Finally Longarm said, "Tomorrow."

"What about tomorrow?"

"A man has t' eat, you know."

"I've heard that, yes."

"Well, I was thinking . . . like maybe you an' me . . . we could go eat t'gether someplace."

"I have a better idea," Julia said, reaching for his cheroot again.

"What's that?"

"There isn't a really good restaurant in Tincup, and believe it or not, I happen to be a very good cook. Why don't you come have supper with me tomorrow?"

"Without anybody there t' chaperone? Likely your father will still be in the doctor's office then."

Julia lowered her chin and peered up at him from beneath her brows. She gave him a feline smile. "I know," she said.

Epilogue

Billy Vail, spiffy in a tuxedo complete with batwing collar and cummerbund, stepped forward and extended his hand. Longarm took it and solemnly shook his boss's hand.

Every deputy marshal was there along with Vail's assistant, Henry, and a scattering of other people from the U.S. Marshal's Office. Even Brian Henry was in attendance, having been pardoned by the circuit judge, who said the young man had shown remarkable honesty after his arrest and posed no threat to society.

"We will miss you," Vail said.

"I think I'm gonna miss you fellas, too," Longarm said, "but Julia's father needs someone to help him watch over their properties."

Billy's eyebrows went up. "Properties? Like in more of them?"

"Uh-huh. They have the gold mine in Tincup an' others in Tarryall and Silver Cliff. I think there's one in Wetmore.

An' there's some unproven claims down around Chama. He wants Julia an' me to go down an' develop those."

Billy nodded. "We've had a good run, Custis. You've been a good deputy. The best." Billy smiled and glanced over his shoulder to make sure Julia was not close. "You've stepped into it, Custis. She's beautiful and her father is rich. What more could anyone want?" He laughed and clapped Longarm on the shoulder.

It was going to be odd after all these years to turn in his badge and hang up his guns, but Aaron needed his help. Or pretended to. Longarm really was not sure which of those two things was accurate.

Still, his resignation had been accepted and his things packed. It startled him to realize how little he had accumulated through the years. He suspected the future would not be so Spartan.

"Dearly beloved," the Reverend Donald Soames began, "we are gathered here in the sight of God, and in the face of this company, to join together this man and this woman in holy matrimony . . ."

GIANT-SIZED ADVENTURE FROM
AVENGING ANGEL LONGARM.

BY TABOR EVANS

penguin.com/actionwesterns

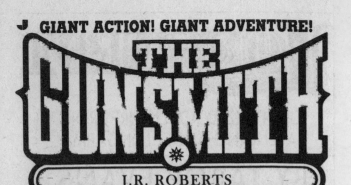

GIANT ACTION! GIANT ADVENTURE!

THE GUNSMITH

J.R. ROBERTS

penguin.com/actionwesterns

M455AS0812